# SEOTSE

A Visionary Tale

Part Three
of
*Green River Saga*

# SEOTSE

## A Visionary Tale

Part Three
of
*Green River Saga*

A Novel

Michael W. Shurgot

SUNSTONE PRESS
SANTA FE

© 2024 by Michael W. Shurgot
All Rights Reserved
No part of this book may be reproduced in any form or by any electronic or mechanical means including information storage and retrieval systems without permission in writing from the publisher, except by a reviewer who may quote brief passages in a review.

Sunstone books may be purchased for educational, business, or sales promotional use. For information please write: Special Markets Department, Sunstone Press, P.O. Box 2321, Santa Fe, New Mexico 87504-2321.
Printed on acid-free paper
∞
eBook: 978-1-61139-756-7

Library of Congress Cataloging-in-Publication Data

Names: Shurgot, Michael W., 1943- author.
Title: Seotse : a visionary tale : a novel / Michael W. Shurgot.
Description: Santa Fe : Sunstone Press, 2024. | Series: Green River saga ; part three | Summary: "Johnny Redarrow, the son of Johnny Redfeather, leaves his railroad job in Evanston, Wyoming in 1889 to seek his father's spirit and, along with Mary White Eagle, renews his tribal spirituality by participating in a Cheyenne renewal ceremony"-- Provided by publisher.
Identifiers: LCCN 2024043474 | ISBN 9781632936899 (paperback ; acid-free paper) | ISBN 9781611397567 (epub)
Subjects: LCGFT: Western fiction. | Novels.
Classification: LCC PS3619.H8676 S46 2024 | DDC 813/.6--dc23/eng/20240924
LC record available at https://lccn.loc.gov/2024043474

**WWW.SUNSTONEPRESS.COM**
SUNSTONE PRESS / POST OFFICE BOX 2321 / SANTA FE, NM 87504-2321 /USA
(505) 988-4418

To:
Three extraordinary women:
Gail Stumvoll Shurgot, Mary Lee Brand, and Anne Martin
and
The memory of Rick O'Shea
The only begetter of Johnny Redfeather

There is a time coming...when many things will change. Strangers called Earth Men will appear among you. Their skins are light-colored, and their ways are powerful. They clip their hair short and speak no Indian tongue. Follow nothing that these Earth Men do, but keep your own ways that I have taught you as long as you can.
 —"Sweet Medicine," in *Cheyenne Memories*

[I]n the Indian, the spirit of the land is still vested; it will be until other men are able to divine and meet its rhythm. Men must be born and reborn to belong. Their bodies must be formed of the dust of their forefathers' bones.
 —Luther Standing Bear, *Land of the Spotted Eagle*

Among the peoples clamoring for religious certitude are American Indians. As they search for religious experiences to help make them whole once again, they discover the fascination and familiarity of tribal religions.
 —Vine Deloria, Jr., *God is Red*

[Men] have set up gods and called upon each other, 'Give up your gods and come worship ours, or else death to you and to your gods.'
 —Fyodor Dostoyevsky, "The Grand Inquisitor," in *The Brothers Karamazov*

## Prelude

In late June, 1867 Johnny Redfeather, of mixed Cheyenne and Irish heritage, retreated to his cabin high on Raven Mountain along with Courtney Dillard, his pregnant lover, and Amanda, his young adopted daughter. They fled Green River, Wyoming to escape the mad revenge of Jake Bulger, whose younger brother Redfeather had killed during an escape from a Civil War POW camp in 1864. Despite Redfeather's best efforts, Bulger found him and killed him. An avalanche, seemingly triggered by the mountain itself, as if angry at the death of Redfeather, and aided by Hestovatohkeo'o, in English "Two-Face," in Cheyenne legends a malevolent simian monster, killed Bulger on his way down the mountain.

On Sunday, June 21st, 1868 Courtney Dillard, her nine month old son Johnny Redarrow, and Amanda left Green River for Evanston, Wyoming, a railroad town west of Green River, in an old buggy driven by Butch Grogan, until then deputy to Sheriff Jim Talbot in Green River.

## Prologue
## July 11, 1869
## Summit Springs, Wyoming

The Pawnee Indians and soldiers in General Eugene A. Carr's Fifth Calvary killed nearly everyone they initially encountered in the camp of Cheyenne chief Tall Bull. The Cheyenne Dog Soldiers, and some Sioux among them, were so surprised by the attack that they panicked, and were unable to defend themselves or the women and children in their camp. Many who attempted to flee were caught and scalped.

Late in the day Major Frank North, who served under General Carr, surrounded a ravine where Tall Bull, two of his wives, his six year old daughter, a few other women and children, and several elderly men and women had fled. After securing his wives and child in the ravine, Tall Bull disabled his horse. This was where he would fight and die. The men dug footholds in the side of the ravine and used them to reach the rim and fire at Major North's soldiers. Tall Bull climbed to the rim and, seeing Major North riding toward him, fired at him but missed. North dismounted, marked where Tall Bull had appeared, and waited. When Tall Bull reappeared, Major North shot him in the head.

A few minutes later Tall Bull's elder wife appeared in the same place at the rim of the ravine holding the hand of her terrified daughter. Tall Bull's wife gestured that she wanted to speak to Major North. He beckoned her to come forth, and when she approached him he told her to take her daughter to the back of his contingent where he said they would be safe. He then released his soldiers and the Pawnees, who hated the Cheyenne, to kill the remaining men, women, and children in the ravine.

# 1
## June 20, 1889
## Fort Laramie, Wyoming

Aided by a stiff breeze blowing from the east, several dust devils carved random passages through the hardy summer flowers blooming among the sage brush and a few stunted trees on the hills above Fort Laramie. The early evening sun baked the large open plain on the south side of the river, where numerous wagons and several Indian lodges stood in silent though tense opposition. Hawks, crows, and ravens, ever wary of the bald eagles that frequented the river and the surrounding grasslands, floated effortlessly on the breeze as they too searched for an evening meal. The Laramie River, indifferent to the swirling dust, summer heat, and aerial visitors, wandered lazily around the southern boundary of the fort before turning sharply north and encircling the western edge of the large military settlement.

The fort's numerous structures, especially those clustered around the central parade grounds, contrasted sharply with the gentle, rolling contours of their surroundings. Rising from the high desert floor north of the river the square, rigid buildings announced their dominance over the landscape, ignoring the land and vegetation beyond them while seemingly insulating their inhabitants from the imagined dangers of the natural world. Housed within these structures were numerous shops and services: a blacksmith, two bakeries used by both white and Indian women, a large dining hall, a general store where travelers purchased supplies, a commissary, a saloon open to military personnel, herders and travelers, a medical facility next to a small chapel, and numerous wooden and adobe houses where military families lived. To the east were several smaller houses, some inhabited by Indian families, but many used by white and Indian prostitutes who plied their trade to soldiers and the travelers who arrived daily with the endless wagon trains.

On a gently sloping hillside just beyond the northern edge of the fort was a burial ground used exclusively by Indians. Beyond that, spread over many acres, were large hay fields that both the soldiers and Indians harvested to feed their horses and to sell hay to the legions of travelers seeking sustenance for their animals. The natural terrain from which the fort had been carved—seemingly endless prairie, meandering river, and rolling hills looming beyond the buildings—had been transformed into acres of alien rectangles.

The main entrance to the fort was from a wide dirt road that bordered the far eastern edge of the complex and then crossed the Laramie River on a recently repaired wooden bridge. Wagon trains traveling this road could cross the bridge and ride directly into the central quadrangle, or turn left and enter the large campground where dozens of Cheyenne and Arapaho Indians in lodges and numerous white families in wagon trains cautiously shared the open ground.

This evening the campground was exceptionally crowded. Three days before ten wagons crowded with passengers seeking rest and provisions had arrived at the fort and settled close to the river and just east of the Indian lodges. Among the travelers were numerous families hoping to join established settlements further west, or perhaps buy a small parcel of land they hoped to farm in the expansive territories west of Wyoming Territory. Also riding in the wagons were many single men hoping to find work as either ranch hands or loggers, or on crews clearing land and laying track for the ever-expanding railroads. Some still dreamed of finding and claiming an undiscovered field of gold in the hills of California that they had heard about back east.

Women prepared meals they would cook over fire pits dug into the ground at the back of their wagons, while small children, pursued by their older siblings, ran helter-skelter around the sprawling campsite. Sitting at the back of one of the last wagons to arrive was an old black man. His boots dated from Noah's time and his soiled denim pants, with ragged cuffs shortened to fit him, bore so many multi-colored patches that he resembled a walking winter quilt stitched together by a hundred different hands. His tattered buckskin shirt, worn out at the elbows and meant for a smaller man, was fastened across his barrel chest by three large pins. A leather vest, missing several buttons, stretched across his shirt and was held together by a short ragged rope. A lopsided, black bowler hat perched so precariously on his head that even a slight nod or a sideward glance threatened to dislodge it. He slowly strummed a dilapidated guitar held together, like his life, with twine and glue. He had carried his instrument with him for several months on his long, lonely, and sometimes dangerous journey.

"Yep, a bullet scraped the corner of this here guitar," he was saying to a young woman from a neighboring wagon. "'Bout two months ago during a skirmish with some Indians back east of here, near what I think is called Pine Bluff or some such place. Wasn't ever sure of the exact name of the little settlement. Cavalry run 'em off after just about twenty-five minutes, maybe a little longer. Bullet came right through the back of the wagon where I stored my gear an' stuff. Just nicked the edge here. I can still play it all right, though. Like to hear a tune?"

"Well, not right now," the woman said. "I need to finish helping my ma get dinner together, then need to clean up after. But maybe after my chores are done," the woman added.

"Well, I guess that'll be all right. I'll look out for y'all later this evening. In the meantime I'll just practice a tune or two I learned back in Alabama 'fore I started up north. I've been travelin' a lot you see since the war ended."

"Yes, lots of folks traveling west now. Looking for a new life I gather. Well, that'd be nice to hear you play later tonight. I'll tell ma and pa and maybe we all can listen to you then."

"Sure 'nough," the man said, and walked slowly back toward his wagon and the family with whom he was traveling.

From one of the large lodges situated on a hill west of the wagons a young, slender Indian woman suddenly emerged and began running toward the bridge across the river nearest the Indian settlement. Shouting "Nahko'eehe, nahko'eehe, my mother, my mother," she raced across the bridge toward the Officers' Quarters at the north end of the fort. She burst into the building and accosted the first man she saw, a young lieutenant.

"Please, the doctor," she shouted. "My mother can't breathe. She is dying. Please! The doctor!"

"Lady, the doctor is not in this building. This is for officers. His office is across the quadrangle at the west end of the fort. I don't know if he is there now. Come with me. I will show you his room."

The lieutenant and the woman ran out of the building to a cluster of small dwellings below a sand bank near the bend in the river. The lieutenant knocked on the door of a small office bearing a scribbled sign "Doctor," and when a man emerged the Indian woman began shouting. "My mother. She can't breathe. You must come. She is dying. Please!"

"Oh for heaven's sake, now?" the man asked.

"Yes," the woman shouted. "Now. There is not much time."

"Oh all right, I'll get my bag and be right back."

§

One hour later, as the last rays of the sun shone over the westward hills, the doctor emerged from the woman's lodge. "I'm very sorry," he said. "I tried everything I could. Her heart was failing, and she just stopped breathing. Her end was peaceful."

"Nahko'eehe, nahko'eehe, nahko'eehe," the woman repeated softly. "She kept me alive when the soldiers came to kill us. They killed my father, all of us in the ravine. Only we survived. And now she is dead. Nahko'eehe, nahko'eehe, what shall I do now that I am alone," the woman cried.

The doctor reached out and held the woman gently as she sobbed uncontrollably in his arms. "You are Cheyenne, aren't you?" he said moments later. "I recognize your words. Where did you come from? How did you get here? Was your father also Cheyenne?"

"Yes, my father was Tall Bull," the woman said as she stepped away and wept. She buried her face in her hands and began shaking so violently that the man reached out and again held her shoulders. For several minutes they stood together, until the woman, still sobbing, freed herself and resumed speaking haltingly. "He was...killed at Summit Springs, when I was very young. My father," she paused, wiping her eyes, "took us to a ravine and tried to protect us, but he could not. My mother said a Major North shot my father, and then she pleaded with him, so he took us away with his soldiers. He kept us prisoners for many months. Later, the army sent us to the Spotted Tail Agency and then Red Cloud Agency, where we stayed nearby for a while with other Indians. Then afterward we had to leave and came here. We stay here with some Cheyenne and other Indians and we work some at the fort."

"How long have you and your mother been here?"

The woman paused, then said "About two years. Oh...." The woman suddenly buried her face in her hands and wept bitterly as her body shook uncontrollably for several seconds before she resumed speaking. "We cook for officers and soldiers, and sometimes for the travelers, and we trade with some of them also. We make baskets, moccasins for little children. Do other things...." She bent over and, clutching her arms tightly across her breast, sobbed again and, grasping for air, muttered softly "No, no, no." She turned from him, walked a few paces away, and stood silently for several minutes.

The doctor stepped toward her. "Young woman, if I...." Hearing his voice she suddenly turned towards him. "Who are you, and how do you know Cheyenne words?"

"I'm Doctor Mark Johnson. I have practiced medicine out here for whites and Indians since right after the war, for almost twenty-five years now, mostly further west near Green River. Two weeks ago I got word that the army needed a new doctor here at the fort, so I left my young assistant at Fort Robinson and came here. Seems this country is getting overrun by homesteaders and all sorts of folks heading west. I learned some of the Indian language from the many Cheyenne patients I have treated over the years. Of course I don't speak it real well, but well enough when necessary."

The young woman moved to Johnson and took his hands in hers. "I see. You are kind. I must bury my mother now. I will clean her body, and gather some herbs to put in her blanket for her journey to Seana, what you call the Milky Way. It is time for her taa'evehane, her journey, all day and into the night. I must find a place for the burial tomorrow morning where no one will disturb her. There is a small plot for burying Indians opposite the river above the fort. She must lie there for four days, and by then her soul will have traveled to its resting place. Will you help me?"

"Yes, of course I will. I will speak to the commander, let him know what we must do tomorrow. I assume you will stay with your mother's body tonight. I will come by early tomorrow morning and we can carry her to a site where she will be left in peace."

"Hah'oo, thank you," the woman said.

"Maha' osane, you are welcome," Johnson added. "By the way, what is your name?"

"In Cheyenne I am Voaxaa'ohvo'komaestse. My mother said my name in English was Mary White Eagle. She said I should use that name when among the whites. I guess you can call me that."

"Well, as you please. Do you need anything for tonight? Are you hungry?"

"No, I am fine. I must be alone now with na nahko'eehe, my mother. Good night."

"Pehevetaa'eva, Voaxaa'ohvo'komaestse. Good night, Mary White Eagle."

## 2
## Burial
## Fort Laramie

At eight the next morning Doctor Johnson approached the lodge where Mary White Eagle lived in the extensive Indian camp. Several Cheyenne men and women, including an older man whom Johnson thought was perhaps a former chief of one of the dispersed Cheyenne bands, stood outside Mary's lodge. Earlier that morning they had constructed a bier of wood and leather straps on which they had placed several old blankets and clutches of sage. The Indians, especially a few young braves, eyed Johnson suspiciously as he smiled and approached the group.

"Pahavevoonao̅, Good morning," he said softly. "My name is Mark Johnson. I am a doctor and fairly new to this fort. I tried to save Mary White Eagle's mother last night. I am sorry that I could do nothing for her."

"Yes," the older man said, "Mary told us that she came to you last night. White man's medicine not much good for Indians. Too late for that now. But she said you tried."

"I did, yes. But her heart failed."

"A Cheyenne woman's heart is always strong. But not forever," the elder man said. "Not forever. But she will be strong on her final journey. And now we must go."

"I told Mary last night that I would help her this morning if she wished. May I?"

On hearing Johnson's voice, Mary White Eagle emerged from her lodge. "Yes," she said to the assembled men and women, "I told Doctor Johnson that he could help. He was kind to me last night. Let him go with us. Help me with my mother's body now."

"Very well," the elder man said. "So be it. Let us go."

Several younger men entered the lodge and emerged a few minutes later carrying the bier. A woman emerged with several of the deceased's possessions, including a large new blanket, a basket, and several shawls and some jewelry. The men distributed the sage around it, and then wrapped it in a large blanket. When they had finished, Mary White Eagle touched her mother's forehead, then signaled that the procession should begin walking to the bridge across the river and toward the Indian burial ground.

When they reached the designated place the men lowered the bier and everyone began gathering stones and small logs on which to place the bier. They constructed a low platform, and after placing the bier carefully on it, the men surrounded it with small rocks, pebbles, and small mounds of dirt and twigs. The women sprinkled sage and other flowers around the bier, then arranged the woman's few possessions carefully around the perimeter. Everyone then stood back. Mary White Eagle knelt by her mother for several minutes, gently kissing her forehead and stroking her cheeks.

"Na nahko'eehe, na nahko'eehe," she muttered. "You saved me when the soldiers and the Pawnee came to kill us. You were hurt by the white soldiers, but you did not die then. You were strong. And now it is time for taa'evehane. I cannot go with you. No'keohtse, you must now go alone. No'kestanove, you and I must live alone now. But you will be strong for your journey, and Maheo will welcome your spirit. Go now. Now no one can hurt you. Not the soldiers. Not the Pawnee. Not anyone! Ever!"

She kissed her mother's forehead once more, then rose and walked slowly back among the Cheyenne. Turning to Johnson, she asked, "How do you know Cheyenne burial rituals? You knew what to do. How?"

Johnson lowered his head. "Years ago," he began quietly, "I helped bury many Cheyenne men, women and even children after a terrible attack on a tribe led by a Cheyenne chief, Running Bear, in Reiser Canyon, north of Green River. Horrible! A Cheyenne man, Johnny Redfeather, taught me what to do, and about the journey to Seana. That was a long time ago, but I have since buried several Cheyenne men and women in the mountains near that town. I'm just glad I could be some help this morning, that's all."

"You were. Again, hah'oo, thank you. Now we must get back. Let us all go together, Indians and white."

## 3
## Fort Laramie

Three days later, after again visiting her mother's burial place, Mary White Eagle walked slowly across the small bridge toward the Indian camp. Just as she reached the end of the bridge a slender Roman Catholic priest, who had arrived at Fort Laramie two months earlier, approached her.

"Mary White Eagle, hello" he began. "The commander told me last night that your mother had died and that you had buried her over in the Indian burial area. I am sorry for your loss."

"Thank you, Father Shannon," she replied. "Yes, Mother is now on her journey to Seana. She is at rest now. No more fighting. No more fear."

"I see. Well, I would have liked to conduct a burial service for her in the chapel over next to the administration building. You recall I have spoken to you often about attending church services, especially the Mass. I wish you would consider joining our little congregation here at the fort. Many of the soldiers and some of the people who arrive here on the wagon trains attend if they stay for a few days. We are not bad people, Mary White Eagle. I know what has happened to so many Indian people, all the killing in the wars for so many years. But I wish you would give me a chance to help you, to help you try to understand Jesus. I've been here for two months now and you barely say hello to me whenever our paths cross, even when we see each other in the dining area. You nod, but you seldom speak to me, and then just briefly. Why? Especially now that you are alone. Won't you need people here to talk to? Can't I help you find peace within yourself?"

"I can talk with Indian people, especially in our own language. And I have Indian prayers to Maheo, the Great Spirit, that I say. Indian people do not need the white man's god, or his religion. I told you this the first time you spoke to me, shortly after you arrived. Why can't you accept what I have said to you?".

"Yes, I recall what you said then. And I know you have your own Cheyenne beliefs and ceremonies. But I wish you and more of the Indians living here would try to understand what I am trying to do for them. The Christian faith can save everyone who accepts it, white and Indian. That is what I am trying to offer you and your people here: spiritual salvation that only Jesus can offer."

"In other places where my mother and I stayed, or were held prisoner, what you call ministers told us often that the Great Spirit, Maheo, was not real and that only the Christian god was real. When I asked them what their god told them to do, they said to convert Indians and to preach to them the gospel of salvation. The soldiers here say that the Indians they fought in the wars were savages. But the soldiers who killed my father at Summit Springs also killed many women and children. My mother saw soldiers shoot helpless young children fleeing our camp. Wasn't that savage also? Like Sand Creek? You know about that attack? Black Kettle flew a white flag. The soldiers slaughtered woman and children anyway."

"Yes, Mary White Eagle, I do know all that. And I am truly very sorry. None of that should have happened. But that was in the past, and most of those wars are over now. We have to try to live together, white and Indian, in places like this settlement here. Jesus preached salvation for everyone, including you and all Indians."

"I have read what your Jesus in the Bible says about loving others, even your enemy. Do the soldiers believe in this Jesus and what he said?"

"I hope so. I don't know for sure about all of them, or their commanders. In war all men, Indian and white, do horrible things. What we must do now is try to prevent more killing. That is what I am hoping to do here."

"I must go now—to pray for my mother's spirit. Goodbye, Father Shannon."

"Good day, Mary. I hope to see you again soon, perhaps at the chapel across the river."

As Mary neared her lodge she saw standing near the entrance the old black man from one of the recently arrived wagon trains. He cradled his guitar against his chest, and as she approached him he doffed his hat with his right hand.

"Excuse me, miss, don't mean to bother you none, but three mornings back I couldn't help seeing you and other Indians carrying your poor old mother to the Indian grave over 'cross the river. I spoke to her for a few moments several days before she died over in the mess hall. You were off in the kitchen I believe, so we haven't had a chance to talk just yet. She told me 'bout losing your father to the soldiers up at Summit Springs, and how you all were captured 'fore you arrived here. I sure am sorry for your loss. I know it's been right sad for you all here, especially now. Like I said I don't mean to bother none, but seeing as how your mother and I talked a bit, I thought maybe you would like some of this old guitar music 'bout now. Course I'm not real good at playin', y'all understand, but I might could make some pretty sounds anyway."

Mary White Eagle smiled at the old man. "Well, thank you for your kindness. My mother did mention that she had talked to you. But right now I think I just need to be alone. I need some time to pray, and think about what I might do next. But maybe some time later. Say, what's your name?"

"Well, my mama called me Joe, though growing up on the plantation the owner called me all kinda other nasty names I don't care to remember. White folks I'm traveling with now, especially the young ones, like to call me 'Old Joe,' so I suppose that's good for now. One thing for sure, I'm no longer young, so I guess 'Old Joe' these days is just about right."

"Well, Old Joe, nice to meet you. I'm Mary White Eagle. Cheyenne all the way." She extended her hand to Joe, who plopped his hat back onto his head so he could shake her hand.

"Well, I sure am pleased to meet you. You decide any time soon you'd like to hear me play some for you, just come on over to our wagon. Course I don't know how much longer these white folks figure on stayin' at this fort, and when they go I figure I'll be goin' with them. Assuming they want me to, of course. Don't really have any other plans, or really much choice I guess. Ain't got much besides these poor clothes and this old guitar. I figure if these white folks get a place they might keep me on to work their fields or maybe tend their animals. Least wise that's what the man told me a few times when we met in Ohio a while back. I told him outside a feed store in this little town I had nothing but was willing to work, so he hired me to drive his second wagon where he keeps all his supplies. He said you'll have to travel alone, but you'll have a place in the wagon where you can eat and sleep. So I signed on, and here I am, way out west. Never figured I'd get to a place like this when I was down in Alabama. Guess you just never know where life might take you, even if you was a slave for a time."

Mary White Eagle sighed deeply as she scanned the old black man's face, noting especially his immensely sad eyes and stubby salt and pepper beard. "Well," she said quietly, " I'm sure that I'll find a time when I would like to hear you play your guitar. It sure does look like it's had a tough life."

"Yes," Joe said, "just like me. We're both old and tough."

"Well, Old Joe, I must pray now. Goodbye, and thank you for coming over to my lodge."

"Goodbye, Miss Mary White Eagle. Sure was nice talkin' to you." Joe tipped his battered old bowler hat, turned, and shuffled back toward the wagons.

Later that night Mary White Eagle heard strumming coming from amid the wagons south of her lodge. "It might be music," she thought, as the vaguely melodic sounds lulled her into a deep sleep.

## 4
## EVANSTON, WYOMING

At four o'clock on Monday, July 2 Johnny Redarrow walked out of the Union Pacific roundhouse in Evanston. He brushed the soot off his clothes, removed and shook his hat, then removed his grimy gloves and shoved them into a back pocket of his oil-stained denim jeans. He walked several blocks toward Front Street and headed toward Harvey's Saloon where he often met other railroad employees, including several from his usual shift. He hoped that a waitress named Julie, with whom he had often talked, would be there. "Maybe time to ask her out," he thought.

As he approached the boardwalk just a few yards from the twin doors of the saloon he spotted an elderly Indian, who he knew the locals called simply "Old Indian Sam," and whom Johnny knew was Cheyenne. He was sitting quietly, almost rigidly, on a rickety chair. Johnny had seen the old man sitting on the same chair in the exact same spot on the boardwalk so often that he almost believed that the man was glued to the chair. His features were so pronounced, and so unmistakably Indian, that Johnny wondered if he might be an embodied spirit come from an ancient Cheyenne tribe. Every visible part of his weathered, bronze face, especially his sunken cheeks, was deeply lined with what Johnny thought resembled tiny fissures in rock formations. Narrow, coal-black eyes nestled deeply in their sockets, and two strands of long, black hair, braided like sweetgrass, hung straight down over his chest. Encircling his head was a wide leather bandana on which were painted red, orange, and blue images of eagles, ravens, and hawks. Inserted horizontally into the back of his hair was an eagle feather, and around his neck hung numerous long strands of yellow, black, and cinnamon beads that cascaded down his buckskin shirt. Over his shirt he wore a leather vest dyed coal black on which were painted several images of buffalos and eagles in vivid red and indigo. Dangling from the belt of his leather pants were numerous eagle feathers and wolf and coyote tails. Stretched across his lap, reaching down to his moccasins, was a buffalo skin robe on which lay a long, slender pipe that he clutched with both hands.

Just as Johnny passed before him he reached out and grabbed Johnny's left arm. He looked squarely at him and said sharply, " Johnny Redarrow, stop! You must listen. It is time. You must go now. You must find the arrows."

"What?" Johnny exclaimed. "Who the hell are you, if you don't mind me asking, and what are you talking about, old man? And would you please let go of my arm. What do you mean? Go where? What arrows? What the hell is all this about? And let go of my arm, will you?"

The Indian tightened his grip on Johnny's arm. "You must seek your father, Johnny Redfeather. I have seen him. You must go to Green River, and then to Eagle Canyon where you will find his arrows. And you must go to the mountains, to your father's house high above the plains. There your father's spirit awaits you."

"Hey old man, you are hurting my arm. Let go!"

The Indian glared directly into Johnny's eyes. "Stop and listen, just for a moment. Just hear me. This is important. Listen, and I will let go."

Sensing a strange intensity in the Indian's voice, and meeting his glaring eyes, Johnny said, "Well, just for a moment, all right. What is this about? What do you mean you have seen my father? He's been dead a long time."

The Indian relaxed his grip on Johnny's arm. "In my visions. I see his spirit, seotse, and it is still waiting for you. You must now find your father's grave, and his house, and then you will find his spirit. Ohtse, go."

"Wait, what exactly are you saying? Find my father's house, his grave? He's dead. I never knew him."

"For Cheyenne, time does not matter. Spirits linger. They are restless. They seek reunion. Perhaps you could have gone many years earlier, but you were not ready. Now you are ready. Go on your journey, your quest, to know your father's spirit."

"Old man, all I know about him is what my mother, Courtney, has told me. That he was named Johnny Redfeather, that he was part Cheyenne and part Irish, how they were together in a saloon and then later in a cabin in the mountains and he was killed by a white man because of something he did at a prison in Georgia during the Civil War. But I know nothing else. And all that was a very long time ago."

"All the more reason to go now. Do not go in this saloon tonight. Go to your mother, speak to her. Tell her you must seek Johnny Redfeather's spirit in the mountains. Tell her also that there is a Cheyenne chief's daughter you must find. She is in a place with many soldiers, and you must go there."

Johnny Redarrow leaned against the railing in front of the saloon, rubbed his sore left arm, and gazed at the elderly man. "How the hell do you know all this? Tell me. Why should I believe you? I don't know anything about you!"

"Hmmm. Maybe not now, but you will. Hataa'eahe, Cheyenne elders, old ones, know. Maheo, the Great Spirit, speaks. Ovaxehene'ena, ovaxevohta'hane. We know by visions, we interpret dreams. Enough. I have spoken. Go now to seek your father. And do not ride the fire wagon. Ride your horse, and walk. Touch the earth as you travel. It will welcome you. You do not have far to go. Peveeseeva. Goodbye. I will see you again."

The old Cheyenne held the pipe aloft, rose slowly, lifted the buffalo robe over one shoulder, nodded, and extended his right hand to Redarrow. He accepted it, gingerly at first, as if still in disbelief, then tightly squeezed the old man's hand. The Cheyenne man smiled, then turned to his right and slowly walked down the boardwalk before disappearing around a corner a few yards ahead.

"Hey, Johnny," a young woman called from the entrance, "are you coming into the saloon or aren't you? You've been standing there talking to that old Indian guy forever it seems. What gives?"

"Oh, nothing, Julie. Not tonight. I'll see you some other time."

"Well, all right, if you say so," she said, smiling. "But I was really looking forward to seeing you tonight."

"Oh," Redarrow replied, "not now, Julie," and turned and walked down the dusty street toward his mother's house a mile away.

# 5
## Evanston, Wyoming

After supper that evening, Johnny Redarrow, his mother Courtney Dillard, and Amanda sat around a table in Courtney's kitchen.

"Johnny," Courtney began, "it's a long way, over one hundred miles. You would have to travel alone. None of us can go with you. Butch is needed every day in the sheriff's office. I asked his wife to ask him to come over tonight after he got off duty, and you see he isn't here yet and it's almost seven o'clock. And he has his two sons to look after. Amanda has her son James and also her job at the general store. Besides, much will have changed in Green River since we left. You probably won't know anyone there. I don't know if Milly is still alive, or Marilee, or Doc Johnson or Sheriff Talbot, or any of the people I knew there. Or even if Milly's Saloon is still open. And who is this old Indian you say told you about 'finding your father?' Or maybe his spirit? I recall some of what Johnny Redfeather told me about Indian beliefs when we were up in his cabin on Raven Mountain, but he is long dead, buried at the bottom of a huge canyon twenty-two years ago. And we aren't exactly living like Indians in this dirty railroad town the way Johnny said we would be for part of our lives. You go to that canyon and all you'll find are whatever the wolves and coyotes have left behind. And that whole canyon is probably full of those damn snakes Johnny was always babbling on about. Scared me half dead he did with that talk. Damn him! And who knows what white people might have done to his grave by this time?"

"Now Mama Courtney," Amanda replied, "don't you go on about those snakes again. Aren't any here. And you know that Johnny just did that to tease you. Now don't go blaming him for that."

"Rascal! Pure rascal," Courtney exclaimed. Sobbing, she lay her head in her arms on the table. "Johnny Redfeather," she cried, and lifted the front of her dress to wipe her eyes.

"Mom, please don't cry. I didn't mean to hurt you by bringing up my father. I'm just beginning to think that this journey is something I should do. Working in that damn roundhouse with those filthy engines every day, drinking in that saloon, chasing white women, white men calling me 'half-breed,' there's not much Indian in my life. That old Cheyenne, the way he looked at me, it was like he knew something important about me and I have no idea what or how. Like he knew my past life. That's downright spooky. Like he was a ghost that's been hanging around my life all these years."

"What do you mean 'ghost?' What ghost?" Courtney exclaimed, raising her head. "Ghosts don't hang around peoples' lives. Or sit outside saloons. That just does not happen!"

"Mama Courtney," Amanda cried, "now stop! No use getting all worked up about this. Your son is just asking. Maybe this old Cheyenne knows something important about his life that we don't. Maybe he knew Johnny Redfeather back in Green River, or maybe even in Reiser Canyon with Running Bear. Or when Johnny was in the war, or traveling north out of Georgia after he and Colonel Swanson escaped from that jail that Johnny told us about. There's a lot of possibilities here that we maybe don't know too much about. I mean there was always a lot about Johnny Redfeather I never understood. Even way back in Milly's before you and he got together. He'd disappear for days and then show up out of nowhere, like he'd been on the moon for a while. Just spooky."

"Spooky or not, I don't want my son going off somewhere he's likely to get hurt or killed. No way of knowing what trouble he might get into back there."

"Mom, stop! Just stop now, please," Johnny shouted. "You're letting your imagination run all over the place again for no good reason. It's like this old Cheyenne has touched something in me that I've been feeling for some time now. I want to know more about my father, and about who I really am. It's not your fault, but I know almost nothing about being 'Indian,' or 'Cheyenne.' You told me about Johnny Redfeather's arrows, about his dancing in a circle at his mountain cabin at sunrise. You said watching him go around and around in a circle seemed really silly, but it obviously wasn't silly to him. You told me that Johnny prayed that Maheo would appoint a star to protect your child. Well, Johnny prayed, and maybe Maheo did that, and maybe there's a star that really will protect me during my journey. And maybe not just for now, but for my whole life. We don't know that isn't true. And now I believe that the Indian part of me needs to know if all that is true, and I believe now it is time to find out for myself. Maybe all this is about what that old Cheyenne was telling me, that he knew it was time for my journey back to Green River to whatever I can find there about my father."

Amanda took Courtney's hand and kissed it. "Mama Courtney," she began, "I think what Johnny is saying is right. When Redfeather took me to Eagle Canyon he showed that he really cared that I knew who my mother was, that she was Indian, not white. And he said that I had to learn about the Indian part of myself, beginning with my name. I wasn't going to be Snuffy anymore, that little brat who chewed snuff and spit all over Milly's saloon. My Indian mother's name was Amanda, so Johnny said that in her honor that would be my name from then on. And all that talk up at his cabin about learning Indian ways. That was really important. Johnny was trying to do what he could to teach me what he thought I should know. And now I think this old Cheyenne Indian is trying to teach Johnny Redfeather's son, your son, about that Cheyenne part of him. And none of that is here in this crummy, greasy railroad town. So, let Johnny go, Mama Courtney. Please! You've done what you could for him."

Courtney Dillard sat back in her chair. She sighed, then momentarily lowered her head and began sobbing softly. A moment later she looked up. "Johnny Redfeather's been dead a long time now, but he's still here, with me, especially at night. He's in my room, and he's always so sweet, and he kisses me and touches me and loves me. And I know I'm only pretending, or dreaming, or wishing, or maybe all three at once, and maybe I'm more than half crazy, but it's all I got now. That and you, Johnny Redarrow, and if you go back to Green River and you die there just like your father did, then what? Then I really will go full blown crazy! Don't you see that? I know living here isn't all that good for you, but you got work and we got money for food and this little place, and, like your crazy father used to say, 'I'll be all go to hell,' but that's something anyway."

"Mama, I could maybe go with Johnny, at least part of the way," Amanda said. "Or maybe Butch too. Might be a good idea to have a sheriff along. Johnny, would you like that? Make the train ride less lonely?"

"Amanda, the old Indian said I should ride a horse and then walk some too. 'Touch the earth,' he said. I like that notion. Working on those steam engines all day all I'm in touch with is dirt and grease and smoke. I know nothing about the earth, not really. So I'll ride and walk, and go alone. I think that's what I need to do now."

"Well, Johnny, if you say so," Amanda replied. "Guess you know what's best about this little journey. Remember what we told you about Milly's Green River Saloon. Guess you could say that's where your life started, where Courtney and your father met. Don't know if Milly and her husband Frank are still there. Maybe try to find some of the other folks we knew there, Sheriff Jim Talbot and Marilee, the woman he eventually married just before we left. And maybe Doctor Mark Johnson. He knew your father in the war."

"Johnny!" Courtney suddenly cried, "If you leave, will you ever come back to me? Will I ever see you again? Please, Johnny, say you will come back to me. Don't just abandon me. Please! You're all I got left of Johnny Redfeather. Dreams and pretending count for nothing! Please, my son, say you will come back for me!"

"Mother, I will return for you. I promise."

"Promise?" Courtney screamed. "That's what your father said up on that awful mountain. He said we'd be there only for a while, and then we would live together, some time in town and some time in his cabin, up there with all those wild animals and those damn snakes! But what he said wasn't true, it...."

"Mama Courtney," Amanda exclaimed, "you have to stop blaming Johnny Redfeather for what happened at his cabin! I've told you many times before, Bulger followed our tracks in the snow. Stop blaming Johnny!"

Courtney suddenly leapt from her chair and embraced Redarrow. "Johnny Redarrow, my son, my son, all that's left of Johnny Redfeather. Go if you must, but come back to me when you have found what you seek. Please!"

"Mama Courtney, I will. I said I would. I'll quit the roundhouse tomorrow, and I'll go see Butch about getting a good horse, and maybe a bedroll. I'll gather some clothes together and head out in a few days. Looks like the weather will be good."

"Well, all right," Courtney added. "Amanda and I can help you get ready. Won't take long. Just remember what you promised me." Courtney rose, threw her arms around Johnny's neck, and wept.

"Mama Courtney, I will."

## 6
## Evanston, Wyoming

Sheriff Butch Grogan was shuffling several papers when Johnny Redarrow walked into his office at noon the next day. "Johnny, what a surprise," Grogan said as he stood and extended his hand to him. "What brings you here? Grab a chair and sit down."

"Much obliged," Johnny said as he sat down. "Well, Butch, I know this will sound strange, but I have decided to return to Green River."

"Green River! Whatever the hell for?"

"Well, yesterday after work this old Cheyenne Indian met me outside Harvey's Saloon and told me that he had received this message, I guess in some vision or dream or whatever, that it was time I went to find what he called my father's 'spirit,' I guess somewhere up in the mountains near Green River. You know, Raven Mountain, where Courtney told me my father was killed by that bastard Bulger. The old man said I had to do this, like it was some kind of destined journey I was supposed to go on. I know this sounds really strange, but in ways I can't fully explain I feel that this really is something I should do."

"Johnny, there's not much for you in Green River. Most of the railroad facilities are here now. You won't find much to do there. Besides, what about Courtney and Amanda? Are they going with you?"

"No, I will go alone. That's what the old Indian said I should do. Even said I had to ride a horse, and walk. 'Touch the earth,' he said. I guess that's important on this little journey, though I'm not sure why."

"Well, I'm not sure why you have to go back to Green River to find what this old Indian called the 'spirit' of Johnny Redfeather, but I suppose if it could be found anywhere it might be back up in those mountains. Sheriff Talbot, who helped bury your father, said that Courtney and Amanda told him that it was a really beautiful place, even if they were always scared of the bears and coyotes and snakes and whatever else

Johnny told them lived up there. But, well, I'm not sure about finding a man's 'spirit' anywhere, especially up on a mountain."

"Butch, I never knew my father, but Courtney and Amanda have been telling me stories about him ever since I can remember, especially about taking them up to his cabin on Raven Mountain where he said he wanted to teach them what he could about being Indian, whatever exactly that means. I know he was mixed, like me, but Mama told me that Johnny said his mother was the daughter of an Indian chief, or maybe a medicine man, and the more I hear about him the more I feel I have to go back to where he was, especially that cabin on Raven Mountain, just to visit those places he touched where he lived. Maybe feel his presence, his 'spirit,' maybe his ghost. Hell I don't know. I can't really explain all of this now, it's just that I have this feeling that what that old Cheyenne said to me is true. That I have to go back, to search for whatever it is that I am supposed to find there. There's not much more I can say about all this, except that I know it really sounds crazy. Oh, and I need a good horse, and also a bedroll. Like I said, I will ride and walk, not ride on the railroad. I was hoping you could help me get ready."

"Well, sure. I've got several good horses that are broken in real well so you'll have no trouble riding one of them. I'll see about it later today. Maybe come by tomorrow afternoon. I'll see what I can rustle up by then."

"Thanks, Butch. I really appreciate this. See you tomorrow then."

"Right. Say about two o'clock. That should be fine."

# 7
# Fort Laramie

Early on the morning of July 4, Mary White Eagle walked across the bridge to the fort headquarters to inquire about securing more wool for weaving the blankets that she and other Indians sold to incoming settlers on the wagon trains. Just as she reached the top step in front of the building she met Old Joe coming out of the large wooden doors. He was carrying his old guitar, and when he saw her he smiled and tipped his bowler hat.

"Well, Miss Mary how nice to see you again. Where you been keeping yourself these past many days? I don't reckon I've seen you since I introduced myself to you back at your lodge after your mother died. That's for sure more than a week now. Where you been?"

"Well, Old Joe, mostly I've been keeping to myself back at my lodge, working some with other Indian women weaving some blankets to sell. Haven't been out walking around the fort like I used to, except on a few really clear nights when I could see the sky where my mother's spirit traveled. Those nights were really lovely and peaceful. I didn't hear you playing your guitar while I was out walking or I would have stopped to say hello."

"Well, miss, truth be told the white folks don't much like me playin' too much at night. They say it keeps the young ones awake, and I can see their point 'bout that all right. But that family I come with is heading out tomorrow, and the man told me he won't be needing me to drive his other wagon no more. Said he got a white man to drive it for the rest of the journey west. So I come here to ask the commander could I maybe stay on here at the fort, maybe do some work for him or the officers, y'all know, some odd jobs here and there. Said I could maybe play some for the officers too, maybe even for the July 4th celebration the commander is planning for later today. He said yes he could use some help an' he said I could stay in this little room at the back of the building here so's I would have my own place. So I'm heading back to the wagons to get my possessions, some few clothes and a picture of my wife that I carry with me. So after all maybe I might just have some time that I could play this guitar for you. Maybe when you have some spare time you might like that."

"Well, Old Joe, yes I think there could be a time for that soon. I got to see the commander about some wool now, but maybe in the next few days, once you get settled, you might come by my lodge again. I just might like to hear you play then."

"Well, much obliged I'm sure. I would like that Miss Mary White Eagle. I'll see you soon then," Old Joe said as he smiled, tipped his hat, then turned and headed toward the dozen wagons scattered around the dusty field across the Laramie River.

§

Mary White Eagle waited nearly two hours before being admitted to the office of Major Stephen Cramer, the commander of Fort Laramie.

"Now, Mary White Eagle, what can I help you with?" he asked curtly.

"Major Cramer, several weeks ago, before my mother died, I and some of the other Indian women asked if you could help us get some more of the wool that we use for weaving our blankets and robes, and perhaps some buffalo hides. You know that we sell the blankets and robes to travelers in the wagon trains and use the hides for leather work. We have not heard from you yet about our request."

"Well, I have inquired about some more provisions for you, wool and hides, but so far I have received no reply. Not many buffalo left nearby, maybe still some further west, but not many here any more. There is some sheep grazing nearby, but I think most of the wool goes to white traders now, and they sell most of that back east for clothing. But I will inquire again, and if I hear about some goods being available I will do what I can for you and the other Indian women."

"We have nothing here. We try to live and to work, but we must now have some help."

"I understand that. I will try to help. But I can promise nothing. By the way, I am sorry for your mother's death. I see Doctor Johnson helped you with the burial. That was good of him. He is a decent man, I would say."

"Yes, I thanked him. He is a very good man."

"Right. Well, I have business I must attend to. If I hear anything more about hides or wool, I will let you know. You getting on all right over there across the river?"

"Well, as best we can I guess. But this is not a good place for Indian people."

"No, I don't imagine it is. Or anywhere else out here now. Thank you for waiting. Perhaps I will have good news for you soon. Oh, and by the way, will you and the other Indians come to the Independence Day celebration later today out on the grounds? We're planning a parade, some music and some games for any children still here among the folks from the wagon trains. Should be enjoyable. You might enjoy it."

"Enjoy it? Really? And what does 'independence,' as you call it, mean for Indians now?"

"Well, out here it means most of the wars between the army and the Indians are over. That seems worth celebrating, I would say. Good day now. I must attend to my duties."

"Duties. Yes, of course," Mary White Eagle said softly. She turned, and walked slowly out of Major Cramer's office. As she pushed open the front doors of the headquarters she saw Father Shannon waiting for her at the bottom of the stairs. She hesitated, and considered going back into the building, but froze when he called out to her.

"Mary White Eagle, I wondered if I might speak to you this morning. I have not seen you in several days, and I have something I would like to discuss with you. Won't you let me accompany you back to your lodge, or at least let me walk with you for a short time?"

She descended the stairs and stood next to the priest. "Father Shannon," she began forcefully, "I told you last time we met, after my mother's burial, that I do not wish to talk with you about, as you say, your god. That is all. Please leave me now. I must get back to the other women."

Father Shannon reached out and brushed her left shoulder as she turned to leave, a touch from which she abruptly shrank.

"Do not, do not, touch me! Ever!" she yelled, and backed away from him.

"Mary," Shannon implored, "I just wish you would give me some time to explain more about my faith to you. Why won't you now, in your time of grief and need, let me explain how 'my god,' as you say, can comfort you and help you find peace in your soul. That's all I ask of you. Some of the other Cheyenne and Arapaho people in the lodges occasionally come to Mass and speak with me about the Christian religion."

"Father Shannon, I know enough about your religion to know that I do not wish to know more. You tell Indians that your god is all knowing and all loving. But if that is so why does he not care for Indian people when he must know that we are being killed by the white soldiers and placed on what whites call 'reservations' with nothing to do and not enough food and clothing? And now some Indian children are being taken from their parents and sent to what whites call 'schools' to learn the white man's way. Why? Why must Indian children be told that their 'way,' as you call it, is no longer good for them? And why does your god not listen when some Indians, as you tell us to do, pray to him and ask for 'blessings'? What blessings has he ever given us? What blessings are there for Indian people now? Why are we prisoners on our own land where we have lived and hunted since before time? Why? Nothing you say can explain any of that to me. So why now should Indian people accept white peoples' god? What is wrong with our god, Maheo, The Holy One? What?"

"He is a false god! That is what is wrong with your 'holy one' as you call him! That is what I must talk to you about, to explain why your god is false, is not a savior or a redeemer, and why you must embrace Jesus and be baptized in order to be saved. Please, let me help you now, at this difficult time."

Mary White Eagle stepped further back and looked at Shannon. Tears formed in her eyes, her lips trembled. Several times she tried to speak, stumbled over words, then, nearly choking, uttered softly, "I see. So that is the final insult to Indian people, the final bullet that you fire at us. Your soldiers kill my father and my sisters and my brothers like wild animals in a ravine, as if our lives are worthless. And now you tell me that our god is also worthless. I see. Thank you for making all that very clear to me."

"Mary White Eagle, I...."

"Do not speak to me anymore! Leave me alone! Do you hear? Alone!" She turned and began running toward the bridge leading to the Indian lodges across the Laramie River.

# 8
# Green River, Wyoming

Johnny Redarrow rode for three days along the rough trail from Evanston to Green River. He camped along small streams in wooded areas where he was sure he would have solitude and be able to sleep peacefully. He heard the howl of wolves the first night, which reminded him of his mother's tales about the wildness of his father's cabin high on Raven Mountain, and surprised a rattlesnake near his bedroll when he rolled over into sunlight the second morning. He threw his boot at the snake before it could coil for a strike, then chuckled as he remembered Courtney's warnings about snakes and how she said Redfeather used to tease her about them. "Damn snakes," he thought. "Sure are everywhere out here. Wait till I tell Courtney and Amanda about this."

During the second night, cool, clear, and moonlit, a fearsome Cheyenne warrior appeared in his dream. He wore leather moccasins, buckskin pants, and across his chest a vest of thick buffalo hide on either side of which were painted images of the sun. In his left hand he held four arrows, two shafts painted red and two painted black. In his right hand he held an ax. Around his forehead was a thick, broad leather band, and attached to the back, pointing upward, were two eagle feathers. He raised the ax and pointed it at Redarrow, then slowly lowered it back to his side. Behind the warrior loomed a gigantic, forbidding mountain, its summit smothered in snow. Two huge, bulging arms of rock and ice on either side of a sheer, glaciated wall beckoned him. As the warrior raised the arrows to his chest a sudden swirl of blinding snow driven by raging winds obliterated the mountain. From the whirling chaos suddenly emerged a humanoid monster so frightening that Johnny Redarrow awoke in abject terror, convinced that the beast was about to tear him apart. Shaking uncontrollably, he scanned his campsite, fearing that it lurked among the trees, but in the moonlight saw nothing. The sudden, piercing howl of a lone wolf startled him, and he curled into a fetal position at the foot of his bedroll and remained there, awake, till sunrise. Just as the sun rose over the hills east of his campsite, he crawled warily out of his bedroll, dressed quickly, gathered his belongings, and began riding cautiously the remaining miles to Green River.

He arrived in town at four o'clock on the afternoon of Monday, July 8th. He walked past the small, battered stage coach office and the larger railroad depot. Several people stood on the platform, luggage in hand, waiting for the next train. Two porters hurried between the platform and the front doors of the depot, carrying suitcases, large trunks, and several ladies' hat boxes. "Must be headed east with all that luggage," Redarrow mused as he walked past the depot and a sign with the words "GREEN RIVER " painted in large green letters and an arrow pointing north. "Seems like a bustling place," he thought. "Can't miss that sign."

Courtney and Amanda had told him to look for Sheriff Jim Talbot's office and Milly's Green River Saloon. Butch had praised Jim Talbot for years as the best sheriff one could ever imagine, and they all remembered Talbot being very friendly to them and to Johnny Redfeather. Courtney had vividly described how lovingly Talbot, along with a woman from the saloon named Marilee and the doctor Mark Johnson, had helped them bury Johnny Redfeather in Eagle Canyon. They had also described Milly's saloon, and Courtney had told him that if Milly's were still standing he could not miss it. "Biggest place in town," Courtney said Milly boasted. "Two story, like a regular New Orleans pleasure palace," Courtney recalled Milly proudly claiming. "Right here on Main Street," as if its location were somehow miraculous.

Leading his horse Redarrow walked slowly up what he guessed was still "Main Street" as Courtney and Amanda had described it. Numerous buggies, carriages, covered wagons of various sizes, and one Conestoga Wagon pulled by ten horses hauling a huge load of lumber rattled up and down the street stirring clouds of dust, and wind gusts scattered tumbleweeds everywhere, creating hazards for a man merely walking. After a few minutes dodging the traffic and barely avoiding young children gleefully scampering back and forth across the street, Redarrow and his horse retreated to the edge of the boardwalk on his right. As he walked he began to sense that Green River was now much larger and more populated than Courtney, Amanda, and Butch had described. Numerous shops of various sizes offering a wide array of merchandise lined both sides of the street for several blocks ahead, and several particular establishments caught his attention.

In the window of the Green River Grocery, at the corner of the first crosswalk he passed, was a sign proclaiming "Open Under New Owners." Unpainted boards on the south side of the building indicated a recent expansion of the business. Next door was a dilapidated, empty storefront, but two doors up was a butcher shop with "Cranker & Son" painted in black letters on a wooden sign above the door. Across the street Redarrow noticed the words "Haggerty's Blacksmith Shop," and "Finest in the West" in two arcs burned into a large piece of yellow pine hanging from a spike above the front door. Taped to the window was a large sign proclaiming "New Location." Next to Haggerty's was the Green River Bank in front of which were parked numerous fancy carriages. "Must be lots of money here," Redarrow thought. Immediately adjacent to the bank was "Burrows Brothers Feed Store & Nursery" in front of which several customers examined rows of plants in small cardboard containers placed on wooden tables.

Directly across the street from Burrows Brothers was Susie's Green River Cafe, advertising coffee and "Fancy Treats," and next door to the cafe was Sara Jensen's New Dakota Bakery. The entrances to both businesses looked freshly painted, and both boasted large signs above their front doors painted bright blue with white lettering. A sign hanging in the window of the bakery claimed that it was "Green River's oldest business." Redarrow wondered how a bakery in a frontier town could boast being older than its saloons. A short block ahead stood Dakota Outfitters, a huge warehouse which advertised "Everything for the Western Man" on a large green and white sign on the roof. Redarrow wondered where the "Western woman" would go for essentials. At the next corner was Jesse Wilkins's General Store, a large, two story building that in the late afternoon was immensely crowded. Seeing an older, portly man wearing a green apron talking to several women just outside the store entrance, Redarrow tied his horse to a hitching post and approached him.

"Excuse me folks, don't mean to barge in, but I'm new in town and I wondered if you could help me find Milly's Green River Saloon. My mother back in Evanston knew Milly many years ago and she asked me to say hello for her. Are Milly and her saloon still anywhere in town?"

"Milly Waters's Green River Saloon? Hell yes it's still in town!" the man exclaimed. "It's just about two blocks up on this side of the street.

It's not quite as visible as it once was, ever since the new city hall and the jail were built right next door. Ha! Seems the mayor and the city leaders and even the sheriff wanted to be close to a saloon, so they built their big new offices right next to Milly's. Ha ha! How 'bout that?" he chuckled. "But, yes, it's still here. You see that big three story building straight ahead, jutting out into the street? Well, Milly's Saloon, as it's still called, sits right behind that. Just keep going straight ahead. You can't miss it."

"Much obliged, I'm sure," Redarrow replied as he tipped his hat, retrieved his horse, and resumed walking north. At the next corner he passed a triangular wooden sign on which were etched a cross and the words "Green River Presbyterian Church." An arrow beneath the words pointed west. "Guess the devil must have a foothold here too," he mused. "Wonder how much luck the minister has saving souls out here. Can't be much more successful than the preacher back in Evanston. Must be a damn lonely way of life."

Ten minutes later, after passing the imposing brick facade of city hall, Redarrow found a two-story building hiding in the shadow of its larger neighbor. After tying his horse to a railing in front of the building, he looked up at an impressive wooden sign painted in bright red cursive letters identifying "Milly's Green River Saloon." Like many of the storefront signs he had seen on "Main Street," the one for Milly's looked freshly painted. "Damn, I bet a man could make a lot of money painting signs in this town," he thought. "Guess Green River has become something of a boom town. Courtney never let on that it looked this prosperous." Rising from the boardwalk and wrapped in bright red sashes were three tall columns that supported the second floor and its wide balcony. The second story windows facing the street recalled Courtney's descriptions of her room there many years ago. On the broad walkway in front of the saloon were several wooden chairs and tables for outdoor dining. Large, clean windows behind the tables opened invitingly into the interior, and peering in Redarrow saw many more tables, equally adorned, and at each well-dressed men and woman enjoying a late afternoon meal. Beer and whiskey bottles stood like sentinels in the middle of the tables. Gazing in, eager to enter, yet suddenly fearful of what he might learn about the town and, more immediately, his father, Johnny Redarrow hesitated.

A moment later he pushed open the swinging doors, and stepped inside. A big clock over the bar at the back of the spacious, crowded room chimed five times just as he entered. "Ha, guess I'm right on time," he thought. Before he could step any further a young, dark-haired woman in a low-cut beige blouse and wide red skirt approached him.

"Hello stranger. Anything I can do for you?" she asked.

"Well," Redarrow said softly, "I'm looking for Milly Waters. My mother back in Evanston, Courtney Dillard, knew her years ago and asked me to say hello. Is she still here?"

"My goodness yes! She's back at the bar I think, probably opening some more whiskey bottles. Seems we have a big crowd for a Monday night. Who shall I say is asking about her?"

"Johnny Redarrow. She knew my father, Johnny Redfeather, and my mother, Courtney Dillard, about twenty years ago. They met here, I guess you might say."

"Johnny Redarrow, well that's a fine-sounding name. Kind of adventurous I might say. You looking for some adventure later tonight? I probably could arrange for that."

"Ah, well no, I..." Redarrow mumbled and lowered his head. "For now I just need to see about meeting Milly and asking her a few things about my father. My mother told me that Milly knew him real well, so for now I just need to speak to her. Could you tell her I'm here, please?"

"Well sure, anything you say for now. There's a small empty table over near that far window. Just have a seat and I'll bring Milly right over. And maybe we can see about that little adventure later on tonight."

"Well, maybe," Redarrow replied, then watched the woman walk slowly away, observing, because he could not avoid doing so, the gentle sway of her hips as she moved. "Been a long three days, riding, walking, sleeping hard. Might be good to have a nice warm bed with her for company," he mused. He walked to the small table, removed his denim jacket and hung it on the back of the chair, placed his hat on the table, and sat down to wait for Milly, still unsure of what he wanted to learn about his father.

A few minutes later Redarrow saw an older, plump woman hastening toward him as fast as her wobbly legs would allow. In her right hand she held a wooden cane which she thrust firmly ahead of every eager step as her entire body swayed from side to side. Long grey hair rolled over her shoulders and down the front of a blue cotton dress that reached to her worn, brown leather shoes. As she approached Redarrow the smile on her chubby face broadened into a grin that consumed her entire face. As she reached for him, nearly tripping over her cane, copious tears streamed from her eyes. Redarrow rose to greet her and held out his arms. She clutched his neck and held him tightly.

"Oh my god! Oh my god," she cried, choking back tears. "Are you really Johnny Redfeather's son! Really? My old eyes can't believe what they see! I never thought I would see the likes of you again after Butch and Courtney rode out of here in Old Willie's wagon. What was it, twenty years ago at least? Land sakes alive, if this don't beat all! Oh how I remember those two together, Johnny and Courtney. She was like to hound him to death the way she would yell at him from the top of those stairs over there. What a pair! And how terrible it all ended. But Johnny Redfeather lives in you, that's for sure! Oh, come give this old shaking lady a kiss!"

Redarrow obliged, then removed a bandana from his pocket and dried Milly's tears. "There, there Milly, no more tears now. So good to be here. Courtney will be glad to know you are still here and running the Green River Saloon. I sure have heard a lot about this place over the last twenty years. Let's sit here and talk. I have a lot I need to ask you. Mostly about my father, but a few other folks too. Come, sit down."

"Good idea! These old legs aren't so strong anymore. Seems I need three legs now just to walk around. Sometimes I lean on my cane so hard I break it. Not like the old days when I could run all over this saloon for half the night." Redarrow helped Milly sit down in a chair across the small table from him.

"Well, Milly, I sure am pleased to meet you finally," he said, and reached across the table and held her hands. "Mama Courtney always says how grateful she still is for your help when my father was killed, especially burying him and helping her tend to me here in the saloon. Amanda too."

"Oh my goodness, that weren't nothing at all. Everybody here knew that Courtney needed us back then. And so now how is Courtney? And Amanda? And what's Butch doing now? My goodness so many years ago you all left here."

"Well, let's see. Butch is sheriff in Evanston, further west where we all live now. He's married and has two daughters. Amanda is quite grown up now, has a young son James, but she didn't marry the boy's father. Courtney is all right I'd say. She never did marry again. Guess Johnny Redfeather was her only true love. That's nice, I guess, but she sure gets lonely sometimes."

"Well, I can understand that all right. My husband Frank died here about three years ago, and I sure miss him around here. We were together a good long time, over thirty years."

"Oh, I sure am sorry about your loss, Milly. Amanda still talks about some of the good times she had with folks here. You, Frank, Sheriff Talbot, some of the women who tried to tame her, and especially Johnny Redfeather. How she took snuff, was called 'Snuffy,' was proud to be Redfeather's 'lieutenant,' and how she used to scare off some preacher who used to come into the saloon on Sunday nights and try to 'save' all the sinners he found here. And of course with her father, Old Willie. She remembers him and a piano player banging out tunes that nobody ever could recognize. She says that Redfeather was the one who figured out that Old Willie was her father. Yes, lots of good memories about this place. So I sure am glad you and your saloon are still here. Mama Courtney told me she had no way of knowing if you'd still be in town."

"Oh yes, this old bag of bones is still carrying on, you might say. The town's grown a lot in these last twenty years you all been gone, but I like to think this is still the only classy saloon in town. Most of the other dumps, like Hal's No-good Saloon up the street, have all vanished. But me and the Green River Saloon still holding on."

"Well, I'll for sure tell Mama, Amanda and Butch all the good news when I return. They'll be pleased to hear it."

" So you all went west when you left here?" Milly asked. "Somehow we thought you might go south. I know Johnny said that Amanda's mother was native from down south somewhere, so we all just assumed that you would head in that direction. Maybe into New Mexico Territory."

"Well, no. Mama told me that Sheriff Talbot had recommended Butch to be sheriff in Evanston, so we headed there right away and once Butch was hired by the marshal they all decided to stay there. Speaking of Talbot, is he still sheriff in town?"

"Yes, he sure is. He and Marilee, who like Courtney used to work here, got married just about three months after you all headed out. Marilee told him she was planning to leave town if he didn't hurry up and propose to her, so he did and they got married. He built a bigger cabin out at Brown's Wash, nice place by a stream. Before Frank died he and I used to visit them for dinner. He says he learned how to cook steaks from your father, and he's pretty damn good at it now. They got three daughters. Real pretty they all are."

"Hmmm. Pretty girls. Maybe I might want to meet them. Never know."

"Well, that could be arranged. But enough of this town. What brings you here after all these years?"

"Well, Milly, this will sound strange, I know, but it's all true. Several days ago, back in Evanston, an old Indian stopped me outside a saloon and told me that 'it was time' to return to Green River to find out more about my father. He was dressed like some of those tribal leaders I've seen in photos of Plains Indians. He was really intense, and while he spoke he seemed to be looking right through me, like he was reaching for something deep inside me. He convinced me that I should come here, to seek to know more about my father. I mean all I really know about Johnny Redfeather is what Mama Courtney, Butch, and Amanda have told me, and I believe now that I want to visit Eagle Canyon, where Courtney told me he is buried, and maybe the cabin where they stayed and where Bulger killed him. The old Indian talked about finding my father's 'spirit,' so I guess that is what I am after. I don't know exactly what the Indian meant, but I want to find out for myself if I can. That's the best answer I can give you. But it's something now I really want to try. House and spirit. That's what I am seeking."

"So you came all the way here alone because of what an old Indian, maybe a wise man of sorts, told you?"

"Yes. When I came home that night and told Mama Courtney about him she thought I was nuts, and she cried when I told her that he had convinced me to begin this journey. It was just the way he spoke, how he looked at me. Something almost, well, spiritual in his voice, his eyes. Not like the preachers in Evanston. Something deeper, like he spoke from some ancient time. I can't explain all this completely, but I was hoping you could maybe help me find Sheriff Talbot, since he knew Courtney and Johnny."

"Well, Johnny Redarrow, your father was the most amazing person I ever met, white or native. His ghost, if I can call it that, still haunts this saloon. All the nights he spent here, how he saved us from an attack so many years ago, he and Snuffy and Old Willie, all his crazy goin' on with Courtney, her yelling at him to stop calling her 'Darla,' his telling her to keep her britches up and be nice. All that. You can be my guest here tonight, and as many nights as you need. Whiskey and steak on the house for sure tonight. We'll see about other nights later. For now, I'll tell old Sam, the cook, to make you a big hearty meal, and tomorrow I'll send you over to Sheriff Talbot's office next door, or out to his cabin if he's not in town. Then you can begin your search for whatever it is you think you need to find. You can fry bacon on that, as I like to say. Now give this old lady another big hug, son of Johnny Redfeather."

"My pleasure," Redarrow responded, and as they stood he enfolded Milly in his powerful arms. He held her for several seconds, and when she broke free he noticed that she was again crying. "Tears of joy, tears of joy, don't you bother about that at all," she insisted. She turned and, waving her cane over her head as if in triumph, hobbled back toward the bar to order his whiskey and steak.

# 9
## Green River

At 9:30 the next morning Johnny Redarrow opened the front door of the adjacent building that overshadowed Milly's Saloon. To the right was a dark-stained, heavy oak door with a large central window on which were painted "Green River City Hall" and "Mayor Jonathan Smitter" in bold black script surrounding an illustration of a river running beneath a towering mountain. To the left was a smaller oak door with "Sheriff's Office" and "Jim Talbot" painted in block letters in the middle of a small window. Seeing a man sitting at a desk inside, Redarrow tapped lightly on the door. The man looked up, then rose to greet him.

"Yes, can I help you?" the man asked as he opened the door.

"Well, yes, I hope so. I am looking for Sheriff Jim Talbot. Name's Johnny Redarrow. Sheriff Talbot knew my father, Johnny Redfeather, about twenty years ago here in town."

"Johnny Redfeather! That was your father? Well, that name sure is a legend in these parts. I have heard Sheriff Talbot mention Redfeather's name a hundred times since I became his deputy. What a surprise! What brings you to town?"

"Well, that's a long story. I came here looking to learn more about my father, and my mother back in Evanston said I should begin with Sheriff Talbot, assuming of course that he is still in town."

"Well, hell yes he is still in town! Been sheriff here for better than twenty-two years. Does a hell of a job too I don't mind saying. Oh, by the way, I'm Jack Creighton, his deputy," the man said, extending his right hand. "Pleased to meet you. I've been here two years with Talbot. Wouldn't want to be a deputy anywhere else, I'll tell you. Come on in."

"Well, thank you. Right pleased to meet you," Redarrow said as he shook Creighton's hand and walked into the office. "Very glad to hear such good news about Sheriff Talbot. My mother, Courtney Dillard, who met my father next door at Milly's, has told me how helpful Talbot was to her when my father was killed, including the burial in Eagle Canyon, which I gather is a ways from here. That right?"

"Yes, that's right. About six miles north-west of town. A short ride, really. Say, Sheriff Talbot is due here soon. You're welcome to sit in the office here and wait for him. Shouldn't be long now. I can offer you some coffee if you'd like. Though like Sheriff Talbot I'm not real proficient at brewing. It usually comes out way too strong. Just grab a chair and sit a spell."

"Well, sure, I'll take my chances. Can't be too bad."

"Well, don't say I didn't warn you," Creighton chortled as he moved towards a wood-burning stove nestled in a small nook to the right of his desk. On the stove a large coffee pot, blackened half way to the top and its cracked wooden handle hanging precariously by one screw, relentlessly boiled its contents. "I suppose one of these days Jim and I should invest in a new coffee pot," Creighton affirmed as steaming coal-black liquid sputtered into two cups. "This one's just plain dangerous to use. One of these days this handle is going to break completely and then we'll have a hell of a mess in here."

"Looks like only a blacksmith could repair that pot," Redarrow laughed as Creighton handed him a cup. "Well, this is sure to wake me up. Thanks."

"You're welcome. I should add...." Creighton was interrupted by Sheriff Jim Talbot's calling "Morning Jack," as he strode into the office. "I see you already have company."

"Jim, we have quite a guest. This young man is Johnny Redarrow, son of Johnny Redfeather and Courtney Dillard, who sent him here looking for you."

"What? What? Son of Johnny Redfeather! My god I don't believe it! Let me look at you. The last time I saw you Courtney Dillard was holding you in her lap, all wrapped up in a blanket, as Butch drove you and Courtney in Old Willie's buggy headed out of town. My goodness what a surprise! What the devil brings you back to Green River? And let me shake your hand!" Talbot extended his hand to Redarrow who put down his scalding coffee cup and clasped Talbot's hand vigorously before they spontaneously embraced.

"When I watched you leave town in that old buggy I never expected to see you again," Talbot continued. "I figured Butch would take the job as sheriff in Evanston, but given what happened to your father here all those years ago I assumed Courtney would never let you come back here. So I am amazed to see you, and really pleased too."

"Well, thank you, Sheriff. I appreciate that. Courtney and Amanda would be pleased to hear that."

"Courtney and Amanda. Yes, I remember them very well. My wife, Marilee, knew both of them at Milly's years ago. And how are they? Oh, say Jack, sorry. We're standing here gabbing away and ignoring you. Johnny, let's all sit down. Did Jack offer you some of our coffee? We take turns trying to kill each other with it. Worse than snake venom. Here, I'll get another chair."

Talbot stepped into the hallway and picked up a chair that he brought into the office. The three men sat down around the large desk.

"Jim, if you want me to leave, just say so. I will understand," Creighton offered.

"Jack, well, maybe for just a short while, if you wouldn't mind. Maybe run over to Haggerty's, see how close he is to repairing that axle that broke last week. He said last Tuesday it would take him about a week. We could use that buggy."

"Sure, Jim. I'll go right away. Maybe stop at the cafe for a bite to eat. Be back in, say, an hour?"

"Well, that should give me and Johnny Redarrow enough time to get acquainted. That'd be fine. Thanks, Jack."

"Sure thing, Jim. See you then. Johnny Redarrow, sure am pleased to have met you. Hope we see each other again soon." Creighton stood, shook Redarrow's hand, then walked out of the office.

"Butch, Courtney, Amanda! Johnny, talk to me," Talbot pleaded.

"Well, Jim, Butch is sheriff in Evanston, married, has two sons. Courtney, Amanda, her son James and I all live together in a house we rent. Amanda works in the general store in town, and her son works for a rancher in the area. Mama Courtney never married. She once told me that after Johnny Redfeather she could never have another man in her life. We have a garden out back and Courtney grows lots of food for us. She also sews clothes for men and especially women, then sells them in town. That and the garden keep her busy. But mainly she's just terribly lonely all the time. 'No Johnny Redfeather,' she's always saying."

"I see. Well, you never knew your father, but I can assure you that he was an amazing man. I can sure see how she would not want any other man in her life. Nobody can compare with Johnny Redfeather. He saved my life, twice, as I am sure Courtney must have told you by now. Once at Milly's during a raid by a bunch of drunks, and then again up at Reiser Canyon during an attack on a Cheyenne camp."

"Yes, Running Bear. Courtney and Amanda have told me all about that. And about Eagle Canyon and Johnny's cabin on Raven Mountain. And what happened there. Neither can forget that. Courtney wakes up some nights screaming Johnny's name. She still sees his body all shot up back at the cabin. I don't think anything can help with that."

"No, I guess not. When you see them again, especially Courtney, please tell them how sorry I still am for what happened back here all those many years ago. But now, Johnny, what brings you to Green River?"

"Well, Sheriff, like I explained to Milly yesterday at her saloon, I am not completely sure. Several days ago an old Indian man, what I think they call an elder, stopped me outside a saloon in Evanston. He told me that in a vision, or a dream, he had seen my father's spirit, and that it was time for me to seek Johnny Redfeather's spirit myself. The way he stared at me, that, well, look in his eye, like he was speaking from somewhere else, maybe a different realm you might say, was so convincing that I decided I had to come here, and go to Eagle Canyon and Johnny's old cabin up on Raven Mountain. So, here I am. I wish I could say more, but right now I can't. Courtney and Amanda said I should start by locating you, since you knew Johnny real well. And I am very glad to have found you, I must say. Mama Courtney and Amanda still talk about you. She also mentioned Marilee, your wife I gather, and also a Doctor Johnson."

"Well, yes, you are right on that score. Marilee and I married shorty after you left. Doctor Mark Johnson left Green River about ten years after Butch and Courtney left with you and Amanda. I think he's worked at a number of Army forts, still trying to do justice to the Indians being kept there. Probably delivering Indian and white babies like he used to do all over this territory. Very good man I must say. I have no idea where he is now."

"I see. Well, I sure appreciate talking with you. I am not sure how long I will be here. Might be a while, might not. I know you're busy, but maybe we can meet again tomorrow, see about visiting Eagle Canyon at least."

"Well, I never did get to Johnny's cabin, so I am not sure exactly where on the mountain it is located. But maybe we can figure that out later. That be all right?"

"Sure thing. I do appreciate this."

"Well sure, of course, Johnny. I'll talk to Jack, maybe deputize another man for the next few days, and then you and I can ride to Eagle Canyon. You staying at Milly's?"

"For tonight yes. I'll see about a few more nights. I've been working steady in the engine shop in Evanston, so I can pay for room and board if she has room. I'll talk to her, then come back and let you know if I will be there or somewhere else."

"Sounds good. Maybe tomorrow we can meet about ten o'clock at Susie's Green River Cafe for breakfast. We can talk some more and make plans for the next day. You probably walked past Susie's on the way here. It's just down the boardwalk. Her coffee is not at all toxic like ours in here. Good food too."

"That all sounds good. Ten o'clock it is. See you there," Redarrow said. He rose, and shook Talbot's hand as he too stood.

"Johnny," Talbot said, "before you go, are you sure about this old man's vision you talked about? You really think he is, well, reliable? And you really think this journey is a good idea, that you will find something important?"

"Sheriff, I don't know right now. What I do know is that the old Indian touched something inside me that I know nothing about. Call it the Cheyenne part that I inherited from my father. Maybe it is time to learn that. Maybe that is what this journey is all about."

"I see. Well, I will gladly help you in any way I can. We'll meet tomorrow."

"Sure thing. See you then."

Redarrow smiled, then turned and walked to the front of the building. At the door he was startled to see the old Indian who had spoken to him at the saloon in Evanston.

"You have done well so far. Go with the sheriff to Eagle Canyon in two days. He can take you there. Look hard and you will find Johnny Redfeather's bones and the arrows buried near the stones that mark his grave. Bring the arrows back with you. Then you and I must go to your father's cabin on Raven Mountain. I will be here waiting for you when you return."

"Old Indian, you followed me here. Why? What do you want from me?"

"Only that you do as you must. That will be enough for me. For my vision. You will see. I will find you when you return. Go and seek your father's bones."

"But, who are you? What is your name? Where do you come from? I ..."

"For now, not necessary for you to know. You may know in time. I must go now, and so must you. Two days." And Old Indian turned and briskly walked away.

## 10
## Fort Laramie

About four o'clock on the afternoon of July 10th Old Joe walked gingerly among the many lodges scattered across the Indian encampment. In his right hand he carried his battered guitar case held together by spindly ropes wound many times around it. Like its owner, it had traveled hard and seen better days. In his left hand he carried a small, three-legged stool.

He stopped in front of the lodge that he knew belonged to Mary White Eagle, sat on his stool, and carefully opened his guitar case. Not hearing any sounds coming from within the lodge, he began gently strumming some chords and humming softly. "Sure is a nice tune," he said to the warm humid air. "Sure am glad I 'membered this one." He strummed some more chords and hummed softly for several more minutes before Mary White Eagle emerged from the lodge and stood, smiling, before him.

"Why, Mr. Old Joe, how nice of you to come by this lazy afternoon. You said you would like to play for me some time, but I never expected you to come by so soon, or to play so quietly like it was only for me. How sweet."

"Why Miss White Eagle, of course it's only for you. Ain't no one else here right now. An' even if there are more people listening, they are sure welcome to listen all they want. But it's for sure for you. No question 'bout that."

Mary White Eagle reached into the lodge, pulled out a wool blanket, and sat down a few feet from where Old Joe was playing. She listened for several minutes, often closing her eyes and just absorbing the placid sounds that he created. After several minutes Old Joe stopped, put his guitar aside, and rested his hands on his knees.

"Miss Mary White Eagle, some few days ago we talked all right, and then afterward when you came out of the commander's office I heard you and the priest, Reverend Shannon, arguing about religion and god and all such. Well, black folk keep on praying to this god, but we do sometimes wonder if he's listening at all. Course slavery an' all that's officially over now, but there was awful harm done to lots of black folks for a damn long time. And some still going on down south. And some of us be thinking maybe we should get our own god, one that might listen to us better than the one we supposedly got now. But I've been studying on all this and it seems maybe we got to wait some more time and be more patient with this god we got, 'cause I don't see evidence that there's another one out there just for black people. Or if there is I sure don't know how to find him. You see my meaning all right?"

"Yes, Mr. Old Joe, I think I do."

"Well, I guess maybe I'm saying that since you got your own god, like you told Shannon, that maybe you and all these Indians, who have also suffered a whole lot in these wars out here, should keep on believing and praying. Seems to me we all got to keep believing in something."

"Well, Joe—may I call you that?— that's really nice of you to say. We Cheyenne people do have our own god, we call him Maheo, the Creator, the Holy One, and we have stories about him and the sacred arrows, Maahotse, and secret places in the mountains and messengers like Sweet Medicine. I can't let some white preacher tell me that Maheo is a false god. To Cheyenne, Maheo is not a false god. He is our only god!"

"Now that sounds real good. I like that sort of spirit in folks. You and all the Indians here, mostly I think your mother said Cheyenne and Arapaho, got to keep that sort of feeling. Y'all never know, sometimes a god can surprise you, just when you think there's no way he can find you. Or you can find him. Works both ways sometimes I 'spect. And yes, you sure can call me Joe. May I call you Mary?"

"Well of course! Thank you, Joe. Nea'ese. Can you say that? It means 'thank you' in Cheyenne."

"Well, I can work on that I guess. That'd be nice, learn some of your language. I guess you know most of mine, but I might dredge up one or two sayings black folks got."

"Yes, that would be nice. Now I got to get thinking about some supper. I and the other Indian women here make supper for some of the fort staff, and even sometimes the wagon travelers, and then we get to eat ourselves. But don't make yourself scarce around here. Bring your guitar and we'll enjoy listening."

"I sure will. Nea'ese. Did I get that right? "

"Close."

Old Joe smiled, picked up his guitar, placed it gently into its battered case, re-wrapped it, lifted his stool and began walking slowly toward the assembled wagons. Mary White Eagle called to several women in nearby lodges that it was time to prepare the evening meals.

## 11
## Eagle Canyon

A pervasive mist enveloped two riders as they headed north out of Green River at 9:30 the morning of July 11. The mist obliterated the mountains ahead of them, creating a sense of unreality about their surroundings. As they passed the statue of an Indian and a white man near the north end of town that Milly and Frank had erected years ago, Sheriff Talbot wondered again about its significance, and his relationship to it, as he had frequently in the past twenty years. He had slept poorly the night before, haunted by his failure to prevent Johnny Redfeather's death so many years ago. Although Talbot knew well the route to Eagle Canyon, this morning he half believed that they were following not that familiar trail but rather a previously unknown path towards an obscured, alien country. "Is this the way to Eagle Canyon," he wondered, "or a path to oblivion inhabited by ghosts waiting to avenge themselves on a white man who had failed to protect the father of the young man riding behind me?" As he rode slowly onward, the image of an Indian, his bullet-riddled body bleeding profusely from every wound, gradually formed before him and floated on the languid air ahead of him. "Johnny," he muttered, "I'm so sorry. I am truly sorry." The grotesque vision persisted until they arrived at the crumbling rim of Eagle Canyon, shrouded in heavy fog that welled up from the mysterious depths below and obscured the canyon's gigantic cliffs.

"We can stop here," Talbot said to Redarrow riding slowly behind him. "The trail down is steep and rocky, and in this fog too dangerous for the horses. We can tie them here and then walk down. Johnny Redfeather's grave is at the bottom near a small stream. I hope it won't be too hard to find." The men dismounted, and Talbot tied both horses to a tall white pine just to their left. Unsure of what more he should say, Talbot stood alone, staring into the huge canyon as a soft rain began falling. Redarrow stood patiently behind him, waiting for Talbot to signal that they should begin scrambling down the canyon. "He knows where my father's bones are located. I do not," he thought. "Guess he has to lead us."

After several minutes, during which Talbot did not turn around to face his companion, Redarrow walked up to him and put his hand on Talbot's left shoulder. "Sheriff, listen," he began, "I think I know why you are hesitating. Courtney told me that you were not able to find Bulger before he killed my father, and that she and Amanda and damn near everyone else at Milly's blamed you for his death. But I don't believe that. I think I understand why Johnny Redfeather took his family up to his cabin on Raven Mountain. He thought he could protect them there, and Amanda has told me about the tracks in the snow that allowed Bulger to find them. And she also believes that Colonel Swanson did not betray my father, that it was the tracks and just some bad luck that Bulger found Johnny's cabin. So she does not blame you, and I don't think that Courtney does now either. Please understand what I am saying. I am not here to blame you or to cause you pain after all these years. I am here because that old Indian told me it was 'time' for me to go on this search for my father's spirit, and that first I had to find his grave and the arrows that Johnny used when he danced at his cabin. No one can change what happened to him twenty years ago. I know that. I don't understand any of this much better than you do right now. All I know is that Old Indian is almost like a ghost or a spirit himself the way he just showed up suddenly, told me to find you first and then ask you to lead me here."

When Redarrow stopped speaking, Talbot turned towards him. "Johnny, thank you! I appreciate that very much, though the past still hurts, especially coming back here. Anyway, we carried your father's corpse down this trail. We'll follow it, being real careful of the slippery rocks. Probably take two, maybe three hours. Let's go." The men began their treacherous walk down the steep, winding trail shrouded in the rising, persistent fog and the light rain that increased in intensity as they descended. "Johnny, we are coming for your old bones. Be there," Talbot whispered to the swirling, indifferent air.

By the time they reached the bottom of the trail three hours later the rain had ceased. Intense summer sunlight had burned through the early morning's mist and graced the walls of the canyon with its warmth. Clumps of cottonwood and pine trees swayed in the persistent breeze, cooling the pungent air. Small streams carved sinuous paths through the sandy ground, forming small pools when the water encountered piles of stones scattered across the landscape. Talbot remembered that they had placed Redfeather's body near a shallow, tranquil pond protected by boulders and debris from adjoining deeper channels. Years of storms and fluctuating water levels had in places altered the course of the stream and carved new channels and eroded some banks. Nonetheless, after a few minutes walking together along a narrow stream near a large cottonwood, Talbot spotted what he thought was the outline of the pond near where they had lain Redfeather's body. The pond was now wider and deeper than he remembered, but it was still protected by boulders and debris from the main channel flowing by. In nearly a foot of water near the middle Talbot spotted the remains of a human skeleton surrounded by stones, with several larger rocks clustered around the skull.

"Johnny, look! Right out there. I am sure those are your father's bones. The pond has expanded and the water is deeper, but the bones seem not to have moved. They still rest where I am sure we left them. It's almost a miracle! Look!"

Redarrow removed his boots and socks. "Wait here, Sheriff." He walked several yards into the middle of the pond and stopped when he reached the clearly visible skeleton. "My father's bones! Old Indian said I must find them, and I have." Redarrow knelt, then reached down and touched the skull bones in the cold, clear water. He then stood and walked back to Talbot.

"Sheriff, you buried my father with his head pointing east."

"Yes. Courtney and Amanda said that was right for Johnny's spirit to go on its journey. I think Courtney said it was to Seana, up among the stars."

"Yes, that is right. Courtney told me you did that. Thank you. Neaése, I think the Cheyenne say. Sheriff, Old Indian also told me to search for my father's arrows. He said they were buried near the stones that mark his grave. But I did not see them. Do you still remember where they were buried?"

"Johnny, Courtney placed them at his head and feet, and also at his sides. I am sure they are gone by now. My god that was twenty years ago!"

"Well, they might still be here somewhere. You never know. The stream might have moved them, especially in the spring when the snow melts and more water flows through. Let's look some more."

Talbot removed his boots and socks and together they walked into the stream. When they reached the skeleton they began carefully moving aside wood debris, sand, rocks and small stones. Redarrow gingerly placed his hands under his father's skull, trying to avoid moving the bones at all. Barely a minute later he grasped a narrow stick, and when he slowly excavated it from the stream bed he held aloft an arrow, its red paint still faintly visible on its shaft. "Sheriff, I have found one. This is where they are."

"Johnny, how amazing! That the arrows would still be here. How is this possible?"

"I do not know. And I do not know how Old Indian knew they would be here. But they are. I must find the other three now. My father's spirit completed its journey a long time ago, and Old Indian said I must bring my father's arrows back with me and then he and I will go to Johnny's cabin on Raven Mountain. So I will now find the others, and then we can leave my father's bones here in peace forever. They have waited for me to find them, and their task is now finished. They belong to this canyon now, and we must not disturb them any further."

Redarrow slowly moved around his father's skeleton. At its left side, its feet, and finally its right side he found an arrow buried under sand, splintered sticks, and small stones. When he returned to the head of the skeleton he stopped, held the four arrows, their red and black paint barely discernible, close together at his chest. He looked up at the rim of the huge canyon, then bowed his head. He remained standing quietly for several minutes, the clear cold stream encircling his ankles, then walked back to Talbot, who waited patiently.

"Sheriff, thank you, Nea'ese, again, for bringing me here. And for remembering where to find my father's bones. I sense something here more than just a bunch of bones lying in a stream for twenty years. Maybe this is where I begin to find my father's spirit, which is what Old Indian said I must do now. It's not just finding this skeleton. I sense that I still have much to learn from Old Indian about my father and about myself. I think this is only the beginning of a long journey, and I have no idea where it will lead."

"Johnny, I am pleased to have been here, and to have helped you in some way on the journey you now believe you must make. I will help any way I can, even if it's not much."

"Sheriff, believe me you have already helped. Now I must wash these arrows in the stream, and then tie them together for our climb back up to the rim. And my feet are getting numb. Let's get out of this stream and into our socks and boots and hike back up this canyon. That trail is steep and will be a difficult hike for several hours. We need to get back to town."

"Good idea," Talbot remarked. As they reached the shore, Talbot extended his right hand to Redarrow. "Johnny, let me show you something. Here, take my right forearm in your right hand, and I will do the same for you. Your father taught me this years ago, after he almost singly-handedly saved Milly's Saloon, and my life, during an attack by drunken herders and rail workers. He said this gesture made us brothers, since we had fought together in a just cause. Because he said that as he held my arm I will never forgive myself for not being able to save him from that bastard Bulger. I deeply appreciate what you said up top about Courtney, and you, not blaming me for your father's death, but that's the truth for me. Always will be."

Talbot squeezed Redarrow's arm, and in response Redarrow squeezed his. "There," Talbot said, "let us think of ourselves as close to brothers now. Let us hope that nothing happens to change that."

"Agreed," Redarrow said, and smiled as he withdrew from Talbot's grip. "Now about those socks and boots."

"Right," Talbot chuckled. "Warm wool socks!"

Five hours later, in summer's soft, lingering sunlight, Talbot and Redarrow reached the rim of Eagle Canyon. Around them now a million cottonwood and aspen leaves swayed to the rhythm of a gentle breeze. Redarrow placed his father's arrows carefully in a side pocket of his saddle bag, then both men mounted their horses and began riding toward Green River. Neither spoke, as if they both knew that now nothing more need be said.

From a bluff high above the canyon, a lone Indian on horseback watched them disappear beyond a crest in the trail.

## 12
## Fort Laramie

"God-damnit, bring me some more beans, and be quick about it," an inebriated man shouted in the Fort Laramie mess hall. "What the hell they paying these scrawny damn squaws for anyway? Ain't I paid for this damn meal?"

In the kitchen just off the dining area Mary White Eagle heard the man yelling and dashed through the door into the hall. A group of cattlemen who had driven their herd to the fort that day had descended on the dining area after spending two hours earlier that afternoon drinking whiskey in the adjacent saloon. The man who was yelling stood on a chair as Mary approached him.

"Hey, you the chief squaw here? That why you came when I called? For christ's sake how the hell does a man get more food around here, especially when he's already paid for it?"

"Well," responded Mary, "you could start by respectfully asking one of the women here to fetch some for you. No use yelling at people in here. That does no good. And Indian women are not squaws, I'll have you know. We don't like that term around here."

"Oh, is that right? You don't like that term around here! Well, mind telling me what term you do like? That might be a way to get a conversation started here," he added as he swayed on the chair then fell against the table as he tried to step down.

"Whoa there, Davis," one of his companions shouted, and several others began laughing at the man as he stumbled to his feet. "You knock this food off this table and you're gonna have a mess of trouble on your hands," a tall, burly man exclaimed.

"This whole god-damn mess hall gonna have real trouble if I don't get more food," Davis barked at his fellow herder. "You ain't ever seen trouble like I can create it, or haven't you figured that out by now?" He turned to Mary White Eagle who remained standing at the end of his table. "And you still haven't answered my question, little big mouth squaw. When...?"

"When you act decent in here, that's when!" Mary spat back, standing her ground with her hands planted firmly on her hips. "And as if it mattered at all to you my name is Mary White Eagle, and if you want to sit down maybe I can find some more beans for you in the kitchen. Otherwise, you can leave now." She turned her back on him and strutted toward the kitchen door.

"Mary what's a god-damn eagle, don't you turn your back on me," Davis screamed, and as he drew his pistol a bullet knocked it out of his hand. "Son-of-a-bitch, who did that?" he screamed.

"I did," a man in full dress uniform shouted from the entrance to the hall. The other herders scattered as the man advanced, pointing his pistol squarely at Davis's head. "And the next one will go right through your puny brain. You get no more beans in here, and no more whiskey at the saloon either. You just get out of here and go sleep off your booze down by the river. We got no room for you anywhere inside tonight. And I'll see to that myself. Now get on out of here!"

"Yeah, an' exactly who...who the hell are you, if you don't mind me asking?" Davis yelled, trying to steady himself on the edge of the table as blood flowed from his wrist. "You wanna tell me who the hell you are?"

"Happy to. I am Major Stephen Cramer, Commander of Fort Laramie, United States Army. That's who! And I will not allow anyone to pull a gun on anyone else in this fort if I can help it, much less someone who apparently was going to shoot a young woman in the back who is just trying to serve meals in here. Now get out! And leave your pistol on the floor where you dropped it. You won't be needing that anymore while you're here. And you won't be here long. You and your herders will get paid tomorrow morning for your animals, and then I'll thank you all to leave this fort. Understood?"

Davis glared at Cramer. "Yeah, I guess so," he mumbled, steading himself against the table and grimacing at the pain in his right wrist. "You win this one, soldier boy," he said, "but jus' you wait, there'll be...'nother... time." Slurring his words and spitting, Davis crept down the length of the table. When he reached the end, he gazed at his bleeding wrist, then tried to walk forward only to fall hard into a chair and then down to the floor. Screaming in pain, he rose slowly, then wobbled past Cramer to the front door and fell into the dust when he missed the first step.

"Somebody go out there and help that damn drunk," Cramer said. "Drag him to the horses' water trough and stick his head in there for a while, then take him to the medicine hut and I'll get Doctor Johnson to clean and bind his wound. Unfortunately, he'll live. But he sleeps outside tonight by the river, not in the bunkhouse. You want your money tomorrow, you do as I say. Understand?"

A gentle murmur from the herders convinced Cramer that they understood and would not cause any more trouble that night. As they slowly left the mess hall, Cramer walked into the kitchen, where he found Mary White Eagle and the other Indian women huddled together against one of the large stoves.

"Ladies, it's all right now. That man is gone. He won't bother you any more tonight. Very sorry about all this. Now please go about the rest of your chores. Good night."

"Commander, we thank you," said Mary. "We will finish now. Pevetaa'eva. Good night."

§

Two hours later Mary White Eagle walked slowly toward her lodge across the river. She was now sharing it with another Cheyenne woman, Ma'o Vahkotseva, Red Little Deer, who called herself Claudia Red Deer when among white people at the fort. Several lodges were clustered together, and in a small clearing nearby several older Cheyenne and Arapaho men and women, and several young children, sat in a circle near an adjacent lodge talking quietly. As Mary neared her lodge she found Old Joe sitting quietly on a wooden stool several yards from the entrance. On his guitar he was lightly strumming several chords that Mary thought she might have heard before, while softly humming along as his voice rose and fell with the melody.

"Why, Old Joe, what brings you here tonight? I thought you might be over closer to the wagons, maybe playing and singing for the travelers."

"Well, Miss Mary, I heard there was some trouble at the mess hall tonight, so I brought my guitar over here figuring you might like some music tonight after all that. Well, 'bout an hour ago this big angry white man, smelling real bad of whiskey and yelling for 'Mary Eagle,' stumbled over here near these lodges, and I figured he was up to no good. I told him you weren't here and asked him could he just go away quiet like, and, well, he just screamed at me, 'Nigger, go away,' and kept yelling 'Where is she?' over and over. Some of the Indian men then came over here and shoved him away, he fell down and then got up screaming god-awful words when Commander Cramer showed up, piston in hand, and said he'd take over. Well, that was that. Cramer said he'd warned him back up in the mess hall not to bother anyone and here he was doing just that, so Cramer marched him off to the brig, said he'd just as soon shoot him as not. So off they went. Well, after all this going on I just thought I'd stay 'till you got back and see if you and the ladies might like some quiet music."

Mary White Eagle smiled. "Why Old Joe, that is very sweet of you. Yes, I believe we would like that. It's getting late so I'll just lie down in the lodge and listen. Claudia Red Deer and the other Indian women will be back shortly, I assume. They are gathering some herbs from the little valley behind the fort over across the river. You just play or sing as you wish, and I'll listen. And nea'ese, thank you!"

"Whatever suits you. I'll keep it real quiet like, maybe play just till the other women get here. Good night now, Miss Mary."

"Pevetaa'eva, good night, Old Joe."

"Oh oh, that one's harder. That'll take a lot more work."

"You will get it. Just practice." Mary smiled warmly, then slipped into her lodge as Old Joe commenced softly strumming and humming along.

## 13
## Susie's Green River Cafe

Johnny Redarrow stepped out of Milly's Saloon the morning of July 14 and walked toward Susie's Green River Cafe. As he neared the entrance of the cafe he again saw, sitting on a chair, the Cheyenne Indian he had encountered outside the saloon in Evanston. The man turned to Johnny and smiled.

"Maha'osane. Welcome. I am pleased to see you again. You have been to Eagle Canyon and found, and touched, your father's bones, and his arrows. Hahtse, you have done well. Now, Peheve'tosane, mano'eetahe, we must do something good together. It is time. You and I must go to Raven Mountain, there to find your father's cabin, his last home among the living. We will take his arrows, and we will make new eagle feathers for them. We will find his hatchet, and with it we will make repairs to the cabin, and we will cut wood for our fire. We will hunt, and the mountain will be generous to us. We shall be a tribe of two, like Johnny Redfeather and his shadow, and we shall pray to Maheo for guidance and help. Two days from now at nine we shall ride, from in front of Milly's. I will meet you there. Today, prepare for several days on the mountain. I will have a good horse for you. For now, goodbye."

"Wait!" Redarrow implored as the man stood. "Who are you? What are you? How do I call you? Where do you come from? How do you know to just show up everywhere?"

"In time you may know more. I am pleased you finally asked my name. Some white people in Evanston call me 'Indian Sam.' Where the 'Sam' part came from I have no idea. In Cheyenne my name is Nahkohemahta' sooma. In English, 'Spirit Bear.' Doesn't sound quite so 'native' in English does it? But if you can't remember all that, for now just call me Nesemoo'o, or 'Spirit Guide.' You can practice while we are together in the mountains. You ask me where I am from. Let us say for now that I am from Ma'xeve'keso, eagle, the great bird, and from memory. Me' etano' ta, I remember. Perhaps you will understand more later. For now ask Milly for some of the provisions we will need. She once helped your father, and she will help you too. Now I must go. Peveeseeva, good day." Nesemoo'o turned and walked briskly away.

Johnny Redarrow watched him for several minutes until he disappeared around the corner of a building two blocks up the street. Redarrow then entered Susie's, ordered coffee and a warm roll with butter and jam, and for several minutes sat in the cafe stirring and occasionally sipping his coffee. By the time he thought to eat his roll it was cold. "What is all this?" he wondered. "What does 'Spirit Guide' really want with me? Guide for what? Where?"

"Sir, would you like your coffee warmed up? It must be cold by now," the young waitress asked.

"Oh, yes. Thank you. I almost forgot I actually had coffee in this cup. Yes, that would be very kind. Thanks. Suppose I had better eat this roll too."

## 14
## Fort Laramie

Around four o'clock two days later Old Joe, his guitar strapped over his right shoulder and holding his stool in his hands, stood outside Mary White Eagle's lodge and softly called her name.

"Why, Old Joe, what a pleasant surprise," she said as she stepped outside. "What brings you here at this time of the day?"

"Well Miss Mary, been a few days since I've seen you, so I thought you might like some little bit of strumming 'fore you get ready for all that work you put in for making supper. I could just sit here on my stool, won't bother no one. You and the ladies just, you know, go on about your work and don't pay me no mind. I be all right just sitting here and playing a bit for you all."

"Well, Joe, I was actually just about to walk over to a grave site here that I like to visit. It's not too far, just across the river and up on the hill behind the fort. Would you like to come with me? Bring your stool and your guitar. You can play by the little mound that is left there."

"Well, I guess that'd be right fine. You sure you want me along to a place like that?"

"Of course, why not? It's real peaceful up there. Some trees. Lots of birds usually flying around. Come on."

Thirty minutes later they stood beside a mound on a hillside behind the fort. A small wooden cross was held in place by a pile of stones, and a bouquet of desert flowers, tied together by a leather strap, graced the tiny monument.

"This is kept real nice. You do that?" Old Joe asked. "This for someone you knew? Your family maybe?"

"No, not really my family. But yet, well, she was my family."

"How do you mean?"

"This spot used to be the grave of a Lakota girl, Hinzinwin, in English Falling Leaf. She was the daughter of a famous Lakota warrior chief, T'at'anka Napsica, Jumping Buffalo, also known as Sinte' Gleska, or Spotted Tail. When she was dying Hinzinwin asked her father to bury her on this hillside, next to the grave of another warrior, Chief Smoke. Some say she wanted to be buried here because she was sweet on a military officer. Don't really know if that story is true or not, but Spotted Tail did as his daughter asked. Later though he had her remains moved to the Rosebud Indian Agency in South Dakota, where they remain. I come here because this is the grave site of another Indian daughter, as I am. Only I never saw my father, Tall Bull, again after we ran from the ravine at Summit Springs, where the soldiers killed him. I like to think that Hinzinwin's spirit is somehow still here, and that her spirit can help me remember my father, maybe connect to him wherever he is. He did not get a proper Cheyenne burial, so I cannot know where his spirit is. I like to think that maybe being at the grave of another Indian daughter might help me find Tall Bull's spirit, maybe bring it here for some peace. There is this English word 'evoke' that I hear. I think it means to bring to a place, or to call someone or something. Do you know this word, Joe?"

"Well, I don't rightly know too many words, never had much schooling. But yes I believe I have heard that word, though I wasn't always clear what all it meant."

"In Cheyenne we say, onoeoesem, to summon. Or onoosetaneva, to call to come. And even moheevohtomo'he, to call together. I think those words might be close to the English 'evoke.' Do you know these Cheyenne words, Joe?"

"Oh oh, here we go again. I was just studying that last word, Pevetaa'eva, good night, and now here comes three more big long words. You sure know how to keep a man's mind busy, Miss Mary White Eagle."

"Well, Joe," Mary White Eagle laughed, "you keep walking around with me and before you know it you'll know more Cheyenne words than you could have imagined."

"Well, that can't be just too bad. Say, think I'll sit here for a few minutes. My old legs are aching after walking up this hill. Maybe I'll just play a little bit. You gonna pray here, sing maybe?"

"Well, yes. I will pray for my father's spirit. Maybe Maheo will help it find peace here some day. And for my mother, who is buried just over there."

"Well, that's real nice. I'll just sit a bit away so's you can be alone. I don't mean to be in the way at all."

"Joe, you are not in the way. I like your company."

"Well, I remember being in church way back when with black folks and hearing some real nice music. Choirs would sing real spiritual songs and a man played a fiddle and sometimes a small piano or even an organ in some of them bigger churches. Maybe I could remember some of those songs, you know, just play the melody like. I can't sing much, but I could play what all I remember on my guitar here. Would you like that, Miss Mary? I sure don't want to bother you none."

"Joe, you are not bothering me! Not one bit. I'll just sit here and pray and you can play whatever you like. I'll listen and I am sure it will be just fine."

Old Joe moved a few feet away from the small mound, sat down, and began strumming lightly as best he could melodies from a few spirituals he recalled. Mary White Eagle sat down by the small mound and caressed the grass surrounding it. She pulled up a few weeds, then opened the canteen she had carried with her and watered the desert flowers that she and her mother had planted shortly after arriving at the fort.

"Hinzinwin, onoosetaneva, onoosetaneva," she prayed. "Ma'hahkesehame, kahaneoohe, kahaneoohe." Mary White Eagle knelt for several minutes, her head down, her hands folded together in her lap. Seeing her bowed, Old Joe struck just one or two strings on his guitar, as if respecting the silence and piety he saw in her. When she raised her head, and then slowly stood, Old Joe stopped playing, stood, and walked to her side.

"Now those words were new to me. Can't know for sure, but I figure they had something to do with your father, like you said before. Am I right?"

"Yes, you are right Joe. I called on Hinzinwin to come, to help me, and then asked the spirit of my father to come close. I prayed to them both, and to Maheo, to let me feel my father's spirit, and to let it find peace. I felt my father's spirit coming closer, but not yet here. I must pray more, believe more. But this visit was good. And I enjoyed your playing. Just those few sounds were lovely. Thank you, Joe."

"Well, it's like I said before back near the lodges some few days ago. Indians and black folks got to keep on believing, even if it don't seem to make much sense. Seems now we got no choice, especially now way out here. Seems sometimes the spirit finds you when you least expect it. And you got to be ready when that happens."

"Yes, Joe, I believe you are right. Thank you for those wise and kind words. Think now we should get back to the fort. Supper time, you know."

"Yes I know. My black belly fixin' to grumble."

## 15
## RAVEN MOUNTAIN

At nine o'clock the morning of July 16th Nesemoo'o, astride a magnificent black stallion, met Johnny Redarrow standing in front of Milly's Saloon. Nesemoo'o held the reins of two other horses, one carrying large saddle bags that Redarrow assumed would carry provisions for their journey. A hunting rifle hung from the saddle of each horse.

"Pahavevoona'o, good morning, Johnny Redarrow. I see by the heavy sacks over your shoulders that Milly has supplied some provisions for us. I knew she would. Good. I have a horse for you. Like your father's, this is a good horse. It will carry you safely up to the top of Raven Mountain. The way is long and steep, and we will ride carefully. No need to rush. You need to see this country as your father saw it many years ago. Touch it. Hear and see its creatures. They will welcome you. Even the grizzly bears, and the great cats, who will have little interest in us as long as we respect their home. Your father knew and respected the creatures who live there. We must too."

"In Evanston I knew mostly steel monsters, all fire and smoke. Horrible! I know nothing of a mountain's creatures."

"Yes, I know. Now you must learn. Take the reins of these horses, load your goods into the saddle bags of the third horse and tie them down, then mount your horse and let us begin. Noohe'se. Much of the forest has now been cut, and the trail to the meadow that your father loved is now easier to find but less wild, less beautiful, so we will ride until we come to the meadow. There we will stop, and make camp for one night. Follow me."

After a gentle ride they emerged from the last remnant of the forest around noon and entered the sprawling meadow below Raven Mountain. A steady breeze descending from the crest of the mountain orchestrated a kaleidoscope of swaying colors: radiant blue of Lupine, Larkspur, Delphinium, and Bluebonnets; vivid red of Indian Paintbrush and Devil's Poker; bright yellow of Balsam Root and Sunflowers; the distinctive Black-eyed Susan; and lighter hues of a thousand Columbine. Further east, toward the mountain, Sage spread everywhere before them.

"A colorful, moving carpet, Johnny, is it not? Almost magic. Your father loved this meadow, and he knew it well. We will ride further east toward the mountain, then make camp, and prepare for some hunting. I believe the mountain and this meadow will be kind to us today."

Two hours later Nesemoo'o stopped his horse and pointed to a grove of large trees to his left, mostly pine with some maple and aspen. "We will stop here, make camp for the night. Seno'o'tse, moheehne. We will camp in the woods together. It's not much of a woods, but it will have to do in this meadow. The trees and those huge boulders will give us some protection from rain and wind if necessary. A short way beyond there is a small stream where we can get water. Tomorrow we will ride to the top of Raven Mountain and find whatever is left of your father's cabin."

"Sure, Nesemoo'o. Whatever you say."

"You've learned to say my Cheyenne name, haven't you? That's good. You now prefer that to 'Spirit Guide' I assume, which I said before does not sound so 'native,' does it?"

Redarrow sighed. "Well, no, it doesn't. But I am none too sure what is 'native' anymore and what is not. Although I am beginning to suspect that the distinction will become clearer pretty soon."

"Yes, it will. That and a lot more. Now let's get camp set up. We need to find some dinner."

Their bedrolls and utensils spread before them, Nesemoo'o and Johnny Redarrow sat together on a large rock with their rifles spread across their laps. They gazed north into the long, wide meadow along a trail that suddenly disappeared, as if at the end of a cliff beyond which was an immense void.

"Looks like if you walked to the end of that trail out there you would just fall off the edge of the earth, disappear into nothing," Redarrow observed.

"Well Johnny, you're reading the landscape. Very good. Not like the inside of that furnace back in Evanston where you repair the fire wagons."

"I am trying to 'touch' the earth, to see it, to hear it. That's what you said to me outside that saloon the first day when you said I must go on this journey. There is no earth in that repair shop, that's for sure."

"For sure. Now, he'kotonoo'e, let us sit quietly, watch, and have our rifles ready. We must wait for whatever Raven Mountain and its meadow decide to provide for us today. Later, tseske'onova, we will talk quietly together."

§

Four hours later Redarrow and Nesemoo'o sat together beneath a towering Ponderosa Pine. Overhead cumulous clouds drifted west, as if pursing the light that painted them so many shades of crimson against the azure sky.

"You're quite the shot, Nesemoo'o. And I must say that somehow that deer meat tasted a lot better than what we get from the butcher in Evanston," Redarrow observed.

"Well, straight from the meadow. No white men between the killing and the eating. Makes a difference I'd say."

"So, Nesemoo'o, you said we would talk later. This meadow is beautiful. Quiet now, here among the few trees scattered around. About all I can hear is that stream bouncing over rocks. Even the ravens have stopped their chatter. Sure is different from everything I have known in Evanston."

"All that is part of why I have brought you here. I wanted you to hear the quiet. Silence is Mo'onevone, a beautiful sound. Vehonatamano'e, this is a beautiful place. Good for talking. Johnny, elders know that much that is essential to the Cheyenne has been lost. The old ways, the language, the ceremonies, like the sun dance. All are being lost. The Cheyenne people, like so many other Indians, are now in forts, or on reservations that white leaders promise to them and then take back later and give to white people. Children are forced to go to 'schools' where they are taught to be 'not-Indian,' to be 'white,' as if you could change the color of a child's skin. They are denied the words I am speaking to you now, even their Indian names. And they are told that Maheo, the Great Spirit, does not exist, that they must believe in the white man's god, who the teachers and priests say will love and protect Indian people even though their soldiers have killed so many of us. Do you understand all this?"

"Yes, I think so. I remember Mama Courtney telling me that Johnny used to talk about Maheo, and about his four arrows that he used when he danced with his shadow up at his cabin. She told me that he said the ceremony was like a prayer to Maheo to ask for blessings, and that he hoped Maheo would assign a star to protect their child. She said that at first she thought he was crazy, walking around in a circle, going nowhere, but later she thought that what he did was really beautiful. Kind of spiritual, she told me."

"Yes, spiritual. Exactly. And that star, to protect their child. You. It will be in the heavens tonight, shining brightly. We will eat tomorrow night at your father's cabin up on Raven Mountain, and we must then begin serious talk the next morning about Johnny Redfeather and his spirit and those arrows you brought with you, and the Cheyenne stories and their ceremonies, and about what must be done for the Cheyenne people. And that morning you must begin to fast for three days. There is a Cheyenne woman you must meet. She is the daughter of Tall Bull, a chief who was killed twenty years ago at Summit Springs, and you two must go on a long journey together. But that is for tomorrow, mahvoona'o, and many days ahead. It is now almost taa'eva, night, and we must get our camp ready. We must stash our food, remove the deer carcass, wash plates, and get the bedrolls out. The sky is clear, no rain tonight. As you sleep, Johnny Redarrow, dream on that star that your father prayed Maheo would assign to protect you."

"I shall, Nesemoo'o. I shall. But first I better clean these dishes over in that stream. I'll also dispose of the deer carcass on the other side, just in case we get company tonight."

"Good. I will stash the saddlebags nearby so we can hear if we get any hungry visitors. Johnny, do you neso'enome, snore?"

"Hell, I have no idea. Why?"

"Well, just deciding how close together I should lay these bedrolls and blankets. You know, old men need their sleep after a long ride."

"Ha," Redarrow laughed. "Well, if tomorrow morning I find you sleeping next to the creek I'll know that I snore plenty loud. I'll be right back."

At the side of the creek Redarrow knelt and began rinsing the plates and cups. After a few minutes he sensed the presence of a creature in a stand of pine trees near a bend in the creek. He stood up, and in the diminishing light he glimpsed straight ahead what he thought must be a huge grizzly bear rearing on its hind legs. Knowing that to run might be not only dangerous but also, in the dim light, foolish, he waited silently, afraid that moving his feet might snap twigs or scatter gravel that would alert the creature to his location. After what seemed to Redarrow an interminable time, the creature began moving slowly away, through the trees and toward the western wall of Raven Mountain. "Hell of a bear," Redarrow thought. "Can't believe it could walk on its hind legs that way. But what the hell else could it have been, big as it was?" he wondered. Once he believed that the creature was not returning, Redarrow quickly finished washing the dishes, then dragged the carcass across a low point in the stream before heading back to camp.

Nesemoo'o had wrapped himself completely in his bedroll, the wool blanket even covering his face. "Out cold," Redarrow thought. "For an Indian who says 'touch the earth,' he sure knows how to protect himself from it. Nothing will get close to him tonight in that blanket. Bet he couldn't hear me snore even if I did."

Redarrow grinned as he slowly slid under the heavy blanket that Nesemoo'o had laid on top of his bedroll several feet from his own. "Not taking any chances on my snoring, are you?" Redarrow asked.

"Nope. No point in that. Everything all right out there?"

"Yeah, though off in the trees I saw something that looked like a huge bear standing on its hind legs. Not certain what it was, but it sure was big."

"Hmm. Maybe a grizzly, or maybe something else."

"What else could be that big?"

"Well, some old Cheyenne still speak of Hestovatohkeo'o, or 'Two-Face,' an ape-like monster that supposedly still lives in these mountains. Could be that, who knows?"

"Monster? Here, now?"

"Johnny, it won't bother us. Go to sleep now."

"Don't know if I can now."

"You can. Do not worry. Sleep now."

"Well, okay, if you insist." Redarrow lay on his back for several minutes. Every time the wind scattered some leaves he twisted around to see where the sound originated, fearful that the creature he had seen earlier might have returned. Once convinced that, whatever it was, it was not returning, he finally relaxed. Gazing at the unfathomable heavens, he wondered which of the numberless stars Maheo might have designated as his protector, and what that could mean for his future.

## 16
## Fort Laramie

After breakfast in the nearly deserted mess hall on Wednesday, July 17th Father Shannon approached Mary White Eagle as she was clearing tables.

"Mary," he began, "would you like to have a cup of coffee with me now? I'd really like to talk with you some more. Please. We haven't spoken now for several days, almost two weeks I believe, and I wish you would listen to me for just a few minutes. I am not your enemy, though you seem to believe that I am. Won't you let me talk to you again, please?"

Mary White Eagle paused, folded up the towel she was using to clean the tables, and stood facing Father Shannon with both hands on her hips.

"Father Shannon, I do not ever recall calling you my enemy, or telling anyone else that you were. You have been kind to me and my mother at times since we arrived, and I appreciate that. But the times that we have spoken about religion, you have always insisted that your religion, which you call Christianity, is the 'one, true religion,' and you have repeated to me that my god, whom the Cheyenne call Maheo, the Great Spirit, is what you call a false god, an idol, whom you say my people should not believe in. And I cannot make you understand why that idea offends me so much. Why can't you allow Indians to have their own religion, their own spirit, their own ceremonies and ways? Why?"

Father Shannon sat down, sighed deeply, and began wringing his hands.

"Mary, please sit down. Please."

She sat down on a chair opposite him, and folded her hands around the cleaning towel. When Father Shannon reached out and touched her hands, she withdrew them immediately.

"Mary, you react as if my hands were poison. They are not. You say you must be free to believe as you wish in your Cheyenne religion, and I say to you that I must be free to believe in mine, and in what as a priest I am called to do. I truly believe that only baptism and belief in Jesus can save your soul, and that without that and accepting Christ into your life as your lord and savior your soul may never find eternal salvation. And my goal in life is to bring everyone I know into this faith so they can achieve life everlasting in paradise with the one true god. And I believe that there is no other way to save one's soul and avoid the danger of eternal damnation, and that all other 'promises' about the spirit life after death are false and therefore dangerous. Only the god of Christianity truly loves all people and can save their souls."

Mary White Eagle's steely gaze silenced Father Shannon. For several seconds she neither spoke nor lowered her eyes. Shannon sat nearly paralyzed, unable to speak.

"Father Shannon, the last time we spoke I said that your god makes no sense to Indian people. You preach what you call the Ten Commandments. 'Thou shall not kill,' you say, yet that is what your soldiers have done to Indian people for very many years out here, like my father in the ravine at Summit Springs. We make treaties, and white people break them, then kill us when we try to defend what we thought was ours. Your government sends our people to 'reservations' far away from our homelands, and puts our children in your 'schools' where they are taught to be non-Indian. I know. I was in one. I asked you last time: 'How is this love?' In the name of 'saving' us, you call us savages and kill us, including women and children!"

Father Shannon glared at Mary White Eagle. "Mary, listen to me! What you say is true, but there has been evil and killing on both sides, including Cheyenne and Pawnee. You know that as well as I do. Most of that is over now, and nothing of the past can be changed. But we can start over, your people and mine, and religion can help us do that. Some of the Indian women, and a few men, come to Mass now. Why not join us this Sunday, when I will say Mass again in the little chapel. Come with the other Indian people, please."

Although the mess hall was nearly empty, some stragglers had lingered over a final cup of coffee, and some few Indian women who cleaned after meals had been listening to the argument as they slowly wiped down tables and swept the floor. Mary White Eagle suddenly became conscious of their attention, and rose from her chair. "No more now, Father Shannon," she whispered, and hurried back to the kitchen and disappeared behind its swinging door. Father Shannon sighed, smiled at his impromptu audience, then rose and stepped toward the exit and out into the yard.

## 17
## RAVEN MOUNTAIN

As the two riders reached the end of the long, rocky trail up the southern flank of Raven Mountain and finally turned north toward the summit, the sun exploded from behind a bank of drifting clouds, bathing the mountain's treacherous west wall and the meadow far below in the soft, fading light of a mid-summer evening. Once he reached the summit Nesemoo'o stopped his horse and turned back toward Redarrow whose horse lagged behind. When Redarrow reached Nesemoo'o he halted, then looked behind him for several seconds.

"That 'trail' as you called it down in the meadow is mostly invisible and really steep! How in blazes did you find that? It looks like it hasn't been used by anyone for years," Redarrow remarked.

"Well, old Indians like me can usually find what they are looking for. White soldiers used to call us 'scouts,' or some such word. In the past wars the American calvary sometimes hired Indians to find other Indians the calvary wanted to attack. Like the Pawnees, who hated the Cheyenne and knew how to find our camps. Like at Summit Springs many years back, where Tall Bull's warriors and most of his family were killed. Not all, but most. So yes, Indians can find trails, even when they seem hoomo'ta, hidden."

"So, what now? Doesn't seem to be much here that I can see. Where up here is my father's cabin?"

"It's quite a ways down in that valley you can see on our right. We ride across the summit a short way, then down through fields of really pretty flowers just below, then down another steep trail to the valley and finally the cabin will appear, almost magically. You'll see."

"And that was my father's cabin? Where Courtney and Amanda said he was killed? How do you know it is even still there after all these years?"

"Until a few years ago some other Indians had been using it as a base for hunting. It's been vacant now for a while, but I believe it is still useful. We won't be there too long, three or four days at most, so as long as it is still there it will be useful enough for us. Now, let's go. We have to get across this ridge and down the trail and get to the cabin in time to gather some wood so we can cook some more of this deer meat. Follow me."

They rode across the summit and through the flowery fields, then slowly descended the steep, winding path on the mountain's eastern slope. The branches of oak trees, cottonwoods, juniper berry, and some huge Douglas firs swayed before them, while vibrant wildflowers, many of which they had seen in the larger meadow below, twirled in the gentle breeze. "What's not to love here?" Nesemoo'o thought as they descended. "No wonder Johnny Redfeather came to this place. Indian paradise!"

Nearly two hours later the riders arrived at Redfeather's cabin nestled amid a grove of tall pine and oak trees. Nesemoo'o dismounted and turned back to Redarrow. "This is it. Let's tie up these horses and get on into the cabin and start a fire. Should check for visitors too. No telling what has been hiding out in this old place, maybe even raising a family in there." As he walked toward the trees he spotted to the right of the cabin door a hatchet firmly wedged into a pine log. "Ah, Johnny's," he thought and pulled the handle up as hard as he could. "Damn, but this is buried deep into this log. Redfeather's arms were so strong!" He relaxed his grip for a second, then, as he was about to try again, he noticed some etchings on the handle. "Yes, the Irish part of Redfeather," he thought as he pulled again and finally freed the hatchet. "I will put this back in the cabin," he decided, noticing that the blade was partly rusted.

He pushed against the heavy door of the cabin and entered carefully. He looked around, saw that it was empty, then walked back to the entrance and called back to Redarrow. "Come on in. The place is empty. No Indians and no other invaders. Ooxhesta, it's just fine for us for a few days."

Redarrow dismounted, tied his horse's reins to a tree limb, then walked slowly toward the cabin. At the entrance he paused. "You seem unsure that you want to enter," Nesemoo'o said. "Why? This was your father's mountain home."

"Yes, my father's mountain home. But it is also where Amanda and Courtney found him shot to death. It's like Johnny Redfeather's blood is everywhere, even inside this cabin. Why should I enter here? This is the place where Courtney said Johnny thought they would all be safe. And they weren't!"

"Yes, I know! This cabin should have been safe, and ma'heone, sacred. Always! But it can be ma'heone again. That is why we have come here. You will see. Now please, enter maheo'o eho, the house of your father. This is the only one he knew in the mountains. Please, come in. We have much that we must do here for the next four days. It is late, and we must eat and then rest for hetomotse' ohe, our humble work. Mano'otse'ohe, we will work together."

"I see," sighed Redarrow. "All right. But I still do not know what you mean by the 'work' we must do. I guess I must believe that all of this journey so far, starting at that saloon in Evanston, is somehow related to this cabin. And to my father. All right, let us go in. If nothing else, I am hungry and it is getting chilly up here."

"Exactly. Just like white people, Indians must be practical at times. Time for a fire and food." As Johnny was about to enter the cabin he noticed the hatchet that Nesemoo'o was carrying.

"What's that thing for?" he asked.

"Johnny, this was your father's. I found it dug into a log outside. His father gave it to him, and these symbols on the handle probably refer to Irish spirits of some kind. The blade has begun to rust, so I will take it inside out of the rain and snow. We will use this to make some repairs on the cabin."

"I see," said Redarrow. "Well, that is good of you. Yes, let's go." And he followed Nesemoo'o into the cabin where they began settling in for the night. Nesemoo'o placed the hatchet on a shelf above the fireplace. "Johnny, I will start a fire. Grab the bedrolls and spread them out on those cots over in the corner. Ha, let's hope they will still support a body all night long."

§

Three hours later Nesemoo'o and Redarrow sat on rustic chairs before a roaring fire that had vanquished the musty, damp aroma of the cabin they initially encountered.

"Johnny," Nesemoo'o began, "tonight we have eaten well, but tomorrow at sunrise you must begin a three day fast. It will be difficult, but I will try to keep you busy so you do not think about hunger. We will talk, about your father and about Cheyenne history, religion, and the ceremonies that are in danger of disappearing completely. We will walk to the valley below, gather herbs and berries, talk about the sacred arrows, and dance out in the sun, as your father did with his shadow many years ago when he had no other members of his tribe and he still hoped and prayed to Maheo. All this we must do while we are here. For now, let us go outside and look up at the stars. Maybe we can spy that star that Johnny Redfeather hoped Maheo would make your protector. Perhaps it will shine very brightly tonight because you are here in maheo'o eho, your father's house."

## 18
## Johnny Redfeather's Cabin

"You have listened well and fasted now for three days. How do you feel?" Nesemoo'o asked Johnny Redarrow as they sat near the fireplace at sunrise on the fourth morning.

"Weak, I must say. Why is all this necessary?"

"You now know more about the history of the Cheyenne people, mostly on the prairies but also in the mountains, all of which you had to know. Our chiefs and warriors, Black Kettle, Little Wolf and Dull Knife, Tall Bull, even Lakota chiefs like Sitting Bull and Crazy Horse, the so-called 'Indian Territory.' The battles, Sand Creek, Little Bighorn, Dull Knife in the Bighorn Mountains, the deadly winter flight from Fort Robinson, Summit Springs, and Little Wolf's surrender near Fort Keogh. Also the army generals, Chivington, Crook, Sheridan, Mackenzie, Custer, Clark, all whose armies attacked and killed our warriors, our women, and our children. We have talked of The Great Spirit Maheo, the Sun Dance, something about the Sacred Buffalo Hat and the Sacred Arrows, though you must soon know more. You also know much about your father, what he lived for, how he tried to protect himself and his family, as he called them. Mostly he wanted to protect the Cheyenne Indian that he knew was deep inside him, mixed with his Irish part for sure, but still in him somewhere. Even though the white man found him, Johnny Redfeather's spirit did not die with his body. Amanda and Courtney made sure that he had that proper Cheyenne burial in Eagle Canyon, so his spirit was set free to wander where it must. And it is here, now, in this old cabin that Running Bear told Johnny about many years ago. Have you felt his spirit? Do you believe that it is here? Or that it could be?"

"The last few nights I think that I have felt something in the cabin besides you and me, something I could not identify. Or maybe I just dreamed that I did. Or thought I was supposed to. I am really not sure which, or even if I am just saying this because that is what you want me to say. I wish I could be more clear."

"Well, you are at least open to believing in your father's spirit, that it is here, and for now, for me, that is enough. Today we must talk more, and then perform a ceremony and pray, and then you will eat. Let us sit outside, in the sun. Bring your father's arrows with you."

Redarrow followed Nesemoo'o outside where they sat on two tree stumps near a scattering of stones. "Many years ago," Nesemoo'o began, "your father made two circles, one large and one small, with the stones you see around here that the wind and the rain and the animals have dispersed. He was trying to reimagine the ancient Sun Dance. Since as a child he did not live among Cheyenne, all he knew of their rituals was what his mother told him, which wasn't much. But he knew that the Sun Dance had been a sacred ceremony to Cheyenne tribes, and when he was here in this cabin he wanted to please Maheo, and so he danced as best he could. He would first walk, then gradually begin dancing around the larger circle, placing one arrow pointing toward each of the four directions. The arrows you hold in your hand, that have magically, ovave, been preserved in a stream deep in Eagle Canyon, are the ones that Johnny Redfeather used in his little sun dance. And because he was alone, he imagined that his shadow was another Cheyenne warrior that the sun created and that moved with him. So, he imagined that he had a 'tribe' of two that performed together a sacred ritual high up in these mountains."

"How do you know all this?" Redarrow asked.

"A few times before he died Johnny visited me near Reiser Canyon after Running Bear had left. He told me that he wanted to preserve his family, especially his child—you—that Courtney was carrying, and that he believed that following what he remembered about Cheyenne praying and ceremonies would help to protect those he loved. Didn't quite work out that way, but he tried. I have stayed in the mountains all these years, waiting for the right time to visit you, to tell you all this about your father, and to begin our time together."

"I once asked you where you were from, and you said, 'From eagle and from memory.' Right?"

"Yes, from Ma'xeve'keso, eagle, and from Cheyenne memory.

Me'etano'tov. I remember. Sometimes that is all that is left, which is why we are here together." Nesemoo'o smoothed the dirt around him with his hands and made two marks with his right thumb, then two with his left, and then a double mark with both thumbs together. He then rubbed his hands together, moved his right hand up his right leg to his waist, touched his left hand, and then moved his left hand up his right arm to his chest. He then repeated these motions: left hand up his left leg to his waist, touched his right hand, then moved it up his right arm to his chest. Finally, with both hands he touched the marks on the ground and rubbed them together before passing his hands all over his body and his head.

"Nesemoo'o, what do all these motions mean? Where did you learn all this?" Redarrow asked.

"From the old ones, from Cheyenne tradition, from what must not be lost. Anyway, about those arrows. There are many legends about the origins of the four Sacred Arrows, the Maahotse, of the Cheyenne. Despite these differences, they all agree that the Sacred Arrows were given long ago to a man called Motse'eoeve, or Sweet Medicine, whom the Cheyenne revere as a prophet and savior. Some stories say he was born to a young maiden in a shelter made of driftwood, and that he performed several miracles that benefitted the people. Some of his miracles created food when the Cheyenne were starving, and the legends say that one day he disappeared over a ridge and was not seen again for a long time."

"When he returned to the tribe he said that he had traveled a very long way to the Black Hills until he reached a mountain the Cheyenne call Noavose, or Sacred Mountain, and that is known today as Bear Butte. Inside a huge room in the mountain he was greeted by male and female gods, and for many days Maheo the Creator and his helper, Great Roaring Thunder, instructed him about what he must tell his people. As he was about to leave, Maheo showed him four arrows decorated with hawk feathers and four with eagle feathers, and he was told to choose which he wanted. Sweet Medicine chose four arrows decorated with eagle feathers, and Maheo told him that he had chosen wisely because the eagle was the strongest and wisest bird. Maheo then instructed Sweet Medicine how to make arrows like those he had chosen, and this knowledge is still sacred to the Cheyenne people today. Maheo then told Sweet Medicine that he must keep the arrows with the eagle feathers and take them back to the people and teach them that the arrows would defeat the evil that was coming to them. So Sweet Medicine took the arrows back to the people. As he was approaching his village, he instructed two young men to prepare for him a great tepee in which he would reveal to his tribe how Maheo wanted them to change and to organize their lives around their chiefs. Sweet Medicine told them how Maheo wanted them to live, and that they were always to keep the Sacred Arrows with the tribe and to choose someone to protect them. And the Cheyenne people did as they were told, and for many years they were blessed with many buffalo to hunt."

"I see. Nice story. And where are these arrows now?"

"The original Sacred Arrows were captured by Pawnee Indians during a battle with the Cheyenne in eighteen-thirty. This was a terrible time for the Cheyenne. Other arrows were made, and two originals were returned, one from the Pawnee and one later from the Lakota. The last time the Sacred Arrows, and also the Sacred Buffalo Hat, had been together was in the Cheyenne village in the Bighorn Mountains in eighteen-seventy-six, when Little Wolf was Sweet Medicine Chief. Now the arrows, the two originals and two copies, are on a reservation in what white people call Oklahoma Territory."

"Nesemooó, I still don't see why you are telling me all this. What does all this Cheyenne history have to do with me? Except for what you have told me, I am ignorant of Cheyenne history, of everything, and I repair the white man's horrible machines."

"Not as ignorant as you were four days ago. One of the stories about Sweet Medicine says that when he traveled to the Black Hills for his instruction from Maheo he was accompanied by a young woman, the daughter of a chief. And now is your part. It is time for the Sacred Arrows to be renewed. Your task will be to take your father's arrows to Hah Ke', Little Man, who is now the Keeper of the Sacred Arrows on the Cheyenne reservation, and explain their origin and who your father was. You will also offer him the pipe I carry, the one I carried back at the tavern in Evanston when we first met. These will be signs to Hah Ke' that you are willing to pledge yourself for the Sacred Arrows ceremony. Hah Ke' will see that you are sincere, even though you are not a chief, and he will accept you. Then he will call Cheyenne chiefs together from far away and explain that they must now perform the renewal of the ceremonies for the Sacred Arrows, for that will renew the spirit of the Cheyenne people. And the young woman who will go with you is Voaxaa'ohvo'komaestse,

White Eagle, who now lives at Fort Laramie. White people call her Mary White Eagle. Not sure where the Mary part comes from, but I guess we'll take it for now. She is the last surviving daughter of Tall Bull, the last chief of the Cheyenne Dog Soldiers, who was killed along with most of his tribe at Summit Springs. Are you following all this? You look a little dazed."

"Well, yes, it's a lot. But why me? And why now?"

"Because you are the son of Johnny Redfeather, who believed and danced and prayed to Maheo to save his shadowy tribe of two. And now you and White Eagle—be sure you learn her Cheyenne name, Voaxaa'ohvo'komaestse—must fulfill your father's wish for the whole Cheyenne tribe. And because I judge you to be worthy to pursue this journey. I will guide you, and be your instructor in the ceremonies, but you must choose to go. Why now? Because more terrible battles are coming, and because the white leader and his soldiers are taking more of our land. And the Cheyenne must renew their spirit to remain strong against all this."

"What do I have to do in the ceremonies?"

"First, be patient. The ceremony usually takes three days, sometimes four. Each day I will be your instructor in what you must do. You must listen to the chiefs, follow many movements in the Medicine Lodge, your naked body will be painted red, you shall feel some pain, fast, dance, wear a buffalo robe, smoke the pipe, chant many words, and help elders renew the sinews, the feathers, and the stone heads of the Sacred Arrows."

Johnny Redarrow looked deeply into the eyes of Nesemoo'o. "You really are sure about all this? I still do not know what or who you are, but you really believe that I must do this?"

"Yes, I am sure. Look, while we have spoken the sun has risen higher. We are no longer in the shadow of these trees. Here, in the light that Maheo has created and sent to us, say that you accept what I have offered you, and that you, like Sweet Medicine long ago, will undertake this journey to renew the spirit of the Cheyenne people."

Johnny Redarrow leaned back, folded his arms, and gazed at the crest of Raven Mountain high above them. "Does this Cheyenne woman, White Eagle, know all this? Will she be willing to go with me?"

"Voaxaa'ohvo'komaestse does not know all of this yet, but she knows about Sweet Medicine and the history of the Sacred Arrows, and she will be willing to travel with you. Both her parents were Cheyenne, and her father was a chief, so she understands that this journey and the Sacred Arrows ceremony to follow is necessary for her people. But she cannot go alone, and neither can you. You two must go together. Come now, decide."

"I am not sure that I really have a choice now, given all that you have told me after bringing me way up here. What if I say no? What if I just want to return to Evanston and those filthy iron monsters?"

"Haven't you just answered your own question?"

"Ha! Very clever. I can't outwit you, can I?" Redarrow snapped as he leaned forward and held his head in his hands.

"Well, probably not. But why would you want to? I am not a puzzle to be solved. I am simply an old Cheyenne offering choices and some guidance, along with some memory of the past and some wisdom for the future. And I would rather not think about what might happen if you refuse this second journey."

Johnny Redarrow stood and walked a few feet away. He glanced at his father's cabin, then at Nesemoo'o, and, after several seconds, said simply, "I see. Yes. I will go."

Nesemoo'o stood, smiled, walked to Redarrow, and embraced him. "Ese-Peheva'e. It is Good. Let us go inside Johnny Redfeather's cabin and eat well, for your fast is over. Then we shall come back outside and use these stones to recreate your father's circles, and then we two shall dance, and with the help of the sun we shall create a Cheyenne tribe of four. Two more than your father had in his tribe when he danced here. See, the Cheyenne tribe is growing. Tomorrow we shall return to Green River, and two days later we shall begin our journey to Fort Laramie to meet Voaxaa'ohvo'komaestse. We could ride one of the white man's smoking monsters, as you call the railroad, but we shall ride two good horses. Touch the earth, sleep on it, eat from it. Maheo shall be good to us, I am sure. Then from there we three must travel to the reservation in Oklahoma to meet Hah'Ke, Little Man."

"I see," replied Johnny Redarrow. "Yes, all right. Let us eat and then dance while we have the sun. And then tomorrow, begin our journey. Yes, good. You must teach me that in the Cheyenne language."

"Vestomevonot. I promise. That and much more."

"Oh, one more question. What about my father's hatchet? Do we leave it here, or take it with us?"

"Hmmm. Excellent question. I had not thought about that. But, well, it was your father's, and is part of who he was. The Irish part. No harm in having it with us, I guess. So, sure, take it with you tomorrow."

"Nea'ese."

"Masetano'ta."

## 19
## FORT LARAMIE

On Sunday, July 21st Father Shannon arrived one hour early at the small chapel next to the administration building. He was to say Mass at ten o'clock that morning for the officers, soldiers, some travelers from the wagon trains, and the few Indians from across the river who chose to attend. Although attendance at the weekly service was unpredictable, even among the reputed Christian members of the military, nonetheless he believed that continuing to offer Sunday Mass for everyone at the fort was essential to his pastoral work. Equally essential, he believed, was his insistence that seating at Mass should not be segregated; he not only refused to designate several benches in the chapel just for officers separate from ordinary soldiers, but also refused to isolate Indians from whites. "All are equal in God's holy church," he liked to say, and he insisted that everyone wishing to worship in his church should enter believing that they had a seat wherever they wished.

This Sunday he was especially pleased because he believed that Mary White Eagle was finally going to attend Mass. Claudia Red Deer had told him on Friday that she had spoken to Mary and encouraged her to come. Claudia had told Mary that she found the ceremonies peaceful, and that in the chapel "There doesn't seem to be any bad feeling anymore between the whites and the Indians." Father Shannon knew that Mary White Eagle hated every soldier and officer at Fort Laramie. "Butchers," she would exclaim to Father Shannon when he tried to assure her that none of the officers or soldiers wished her harm, and that she was now safe at the fort. But apparently Claudia, though equally hostile to the military, had persuaded Mary to come to the service this Sunday. "See for herself," she had told Mary. "Just this once. What else can we do now? So many are dead." She had assured Mary that she would be safe in the company of other Cheyenne men and women, as well as a few Indians from other tribes.

Father Shannon was eager to convince Mary White Eagle of the spiritual truths of Christianity precisely because of her fierce resistance to his overtures and because she clung so tenaciously to her Cheyenne beliefs. Alone in his small room the night before he had prayed that God would grant him the strength and the wisdom to convert her and thus save her soul. "If I can save her," he had convinced himself, "I can save anyone out here in this desolate, savage place. Anyone! To me shall fall the honor and the glory for her conversion, and recognition of my spiritual powers will surely follow." He had knelt on the rough floor of his room, and bowed before the crucifix nailed to the wall above his bed. "Lord," he had cried aloud, "help me to do your work here. Help me to remove the blinders from this woman's eyes, and make her see that only by embracing your sacrifice and my teachings can she save her immortal soul. With her as my companion I can save many more souls for your kingdom in heaven, and we can create from this wild place a true garden of salvation for all people. Help me, O Lord, to secure her for my righteous ministry."

At 9:30 in the meager sacristy at the back of the chapel Father Shannon stood facing the mirror he had set atop his small dressing table. Hanging to his right were the vestments for Mass, the donning of which he considered a sacred ceremony. He followed carefully the prescribed order: first, he pulled the white linen Alb over his head and down the full length of his body; then, he tied the Cincture tightly around his waist; next, he draped the embossed purple and gold Chasuble over his shoulders; finally, he held the Stole aloft with both hands, bowed to it, kissed it, then placed it around his neck so that it hung evenly on both sides of the Chasuble. Satisfied with the ritual, he gazed into the mirror and smiled at his imposing appearance. "Perfect," he thought. "This shall win her to God, and to me."

As he would begin Mass in less than thirty minutes he decided to save time by lighting the candles now so that he would have as much time as possible to greet attendees as they entered the chapel. He walked to the wooden altar and placed two large burning candles in their holders at either end. He then walked past the ten rows of pine benches and headed toward the chapel door where he waited anxiously for his parishioners, as he called them. He was sure that Mary White Eagle would be among them.

People began entering the chapel about fifteen minutes later. Among them were several officers and enlisted men, and about a dozen settlers from two recently arrived wagon trains. Four Indian women and two Indian men arrived shortly thereafter, and Father Shannon greeted them warmly, bowing slightly to the women and offering his hand to the men, some of whom returned the gesture. Just before ten o'clock, when Mary and Claudia had not appeared, Father Shannon was about to turn aside when he saw them, along with Old Joe, ambling towards him. He was immensely pleased to see the women, but wondered why Joe was with them, as Fr. Shannon had not seen him in his chapel previously. However, he smiled as they approached and extended his open hands toward them.

"Well my goodness!" he exclaimed. "How very nice to see you fine folks. Welcome to my chapel, all of you. Joe, a nice surprise to see you here. And Claudia, I see you have brought a friend. How very kind of you. Mary White Eagle, you decided to attend this bright and lovely day of the Lord. I am very pleased to see you here, believe me."

"Father Shannon, I am here only because Claudia encouraged me to attend, and I brought along Joe as well because he has been kind and friendly to me. I want these people with me this morning."

"Well, but of course, Mary. All are welcome here. Please come inside and find a seat. I believe there is space in one of the benches up front."

"We'll sit where the Indians usually do," said Claudia. "At the back."

"Well," responded Father Shannon, "I was going to offer you seats up closer to the altar, closer to God you might say, especially as this is Mary White Eagle's first time here."

"The usual is fine, thank you," Claudia answered, as they walked past him.

"We'll sit here," Claudia said to her companions as first she, then Joe, and finally Mary sat down at the end of the last bench where several other Indians were already seated. As Father Shannon walked past them toward the altar he lightly touched Mary's left shoulder and smiled at her. She flinched, looked up, and glared at him.

He had decided that this Sunday he would diverge from his usual practice and devise a sermon that included carefully chosen excerpts from both the Old and New Testament. Using the King James Bible, which he valued for its beautiful prose, he had woven together what he thought was a seamless web of verses whose lyricism would not only impress Mary but also convince her of the truth of Christian faith. As he concluded the initial prayers of the Mass he thought of her at the back of the chapel watching his gestures and listening to his powerful voice, and as he prepared to deliver his novel sermon he paused to adjust again the Stole around his neck. "Must hang evenly," he thought.

Turning to face the congregation, he cleared his throat, then stepped to the crude podium on his left on which rested the Bible. He had marked with paper the specific passages from which he would read. He opened the Bible first to Ecclesiastes, then looked around the chapel and smiled broadly.

"Welcome, welcome all my friends, to this humble house of God. Our chapel is small and barren, but surely by your presence here this fine morning you show how great is your love of the Lord. And surely the Lord will return that love, for, as we read in Matthew, 'Where two or three are gathered in my name, there am I in the midst of them.' And certainly all are gathered here in the name of our Lord and his son Jesus Christ, through whom we are forgiven our sins and offered eternal life. Amen." He looked directly at Mary, smiled again, then proclaimed, "Let us read and consider first these beautiful passages from the Book of Ecclesiastes, chapter three:

> "To everything there is a season, and a time to every purpose under the heaven. A time to be born, and a time to die; a time to plant, and a time to pluck up that which is planted. A time to kill, and a time to build up. A time to weep, and a time to laugh; a time to mourn, and a time to dance."

He stopped, paused slightly, then observed the soldiers and settlers in the front rows and especially the Indians and Joe in the back. His gaze stopped at Mary, who, avoiding his eyes, deliberately looked down at the battered floor boards.

"Let us consider further these wise words from Ecclesiastes, the Preacher," he continued. "The writer tells us that all things have their proper time and place, including the time of accepting God's holy word and embracing the salvation that Jesus has made possible. For consider also verse seventeen: 'I said in my heart, God shall judge the righteous and the wicked.' Surely then," he continued, "since we know that God shall judge, we should all wish to be among the righteous, not the wicked. For to be among the wicked is to die eternally, and, as we read in Exodus twenty, 'I am the Lord thy God, which have brought thee out of the land of Egypt, out of the house of bondage. Thou shalt have no other gods before me.'"

Suddenly feeling tension rising in the chapel, he looked up and saw several of the Indians stirring in their pews. Mary White Eagle, now glaring intently at him, sat rigidly and locked her arms across her chest. Believing that she was fully attentive, he raised his voice. "Consider now the life-giving words of the twenty-third Psalm," he intoned, looking straight at her. "'The Lord is my shepherd, I shall not want. He maketh me to lie down in green pastures: he leadeth me beside the still waters. He restoreth my soul: he leadeth me in the paths of righteousness for his name's sake.'"

As he finished, Mary was breathing heavily, but she did not move. Confidant that her reaction meant that he was reaching deeply into her soul, Father Shannon continued. "Let us turn now to the New Testament and the words of our Lord and Savior Jesus Christ. In John, chapter fourteen, Jesus says to his disciples: 'Let not your heart be troubled: ye believe in God, believe also in me. In my Father's house there are many mansions: if it were not so, I would have told you. I go to prepare a place for you.' And as I Corinthians says: 'But as it is written, Eye hath not seen, nor ear heard, neither have entered into the heart of man, the things which God hath prepared for them that love him.'"

Staring directly at Mary, Father Shannon believed that his words were beginning to affect her deeply. He closed the Bible, stepped from behind the podium, and approached the first bench. He stood solemnly for several seconds holding his hands before his chest, then looked up and smiled broadly.

"Now, my friends, let us listen to the words of Matthew, chapter five, one of the most profound passages of the New Testament. From the beginning of my ministry these words have been crucial to my faith, and so I have committed them to memory. Please listen carefully to the words of Jesus as he preaches to his apostles." He stretched his right arm over the little congregation, then began speaking slowly, solemnly:

"And seeing the multitudes, he went up into a mountain: and when he was set, his disciples came unto him:

And he opened his mouth, and taught them, saying,

Blessed are the poor in spirit: for their's is the kingdom of heaven.

Blessed are they that mourn: for they shall be comforted.

Blessed are the meek: for they shall inherit the earth.

Blessed are they which do hunger and thirst after righteousness: for they shall be filled.

Blessed are the merciful: for they shall obtain mercy.

Blessed are the pure in heart: for they shall see God."

Father Shannon paused. Just as he had hoped, his nuanced recitation of Matthew's poetic passages had elicited rapt attention among his listeners. He looked over them and, sensing the gravity of the moment, said quietly, "It's the next sentence from Jesus in Matthew's Gospel that is so meaningful here."

He began walking slowly down the narrow aisle toward the back of the chapel. Upon reaching the bench where the Indians sat, he stopped and, sensing hostility, if not fear in Mary's eyes, he gently touched her left shoulder and said softly, "Mary, please, do not be angry. Listen to what Jesus says next: 'Blessed are the peacemakers: for they shall be called the children of God.'"

She stood immediately. "How dare you touch me! I told you never to do that again," she shouted. Everyone in the chapel turned toward the back, and Claudia reached across Joe and grabbed Mary's right arm.

"Mary, please! He meant no harm I am sure. He was speaking of peace."

"Peace! Peace! After what the soldiers did to my father! To the Cheyenne all over this land that used to be ours! Don't you talk to me of peace, Claudia Ma'o Vaotseva! Don't you dare do that! Don't you see what this 'priest' is trying to do?"

Her fury rising, she turned toward Shannon. "How can white men talk of peace after the slaughter of so many Indian people? No, no, they cannot mean peace! They want to destroy all Indians completely!" She pulled her arm away from Claudia and pushed her down onto the bench. "Leave me alone!" she screamed. Joe stood and thrust his arms between them.

"Miss Mary, please now. This here's a church, you know, where folks got to be real nice to one another. Please!"

Amid the sudden commotion Major Cramer and another officer quickly approached Father Shannon. Cramer stepped between Shannon and Mary, and the other officer held out his hands before her.

"Don't you touch me either! Do you hear?"

"Lady, I was not going to touch you. I am just trying to prevent anyone from getting hurt here. Please try to understand that."

"Mary," Shannon implored, standing next to Major Cramer, "for heaven's sake, why won't you at least listen to what I am saying to you? I am offering you, in a very gentle way in this little chapel, the means of saving your eternal soul. Why can't you listen to what Jesus told his disciples on the mountain?"

"Mountains? Mountains!" she raged. "Don't talk to me of mountains! We have our own, and our own savior, Motse' eoeve, Sweet Medicine, and our own religion and our own faith," she shouted at Shannon. "And nothing can change that or make me believe in your 'savior' as you call him. What did the soldiers who supposedly believed in him do to Indian people? To my father? Shot them all, men, women, children! All!"

Crying and shaking, she sat down on the bench. Joe and Claudia embraced her as she cried "No ! No! No!" and buried her face in her hands.

As the parishioners crowded near the back, gaping at the chaos, Major Cramer moved Shannon away from the benches. "Father, I think this service is over. Please send everyone away now."

"Yes, I guess you are right. Very well." He turned toward the congregation gathered near him. "Please, all go home now, back to your work or your residences. That is all for today. Thank you." He looked at Mary, her head down, still sitting and weeping, then walked to the back of the chapel, picked up the Bible from the podium, and disappeared into the sacristy.

"All right now, everyone just forget this little episode," Major Cramer said calmly. "Go on home now. Have a peaceful day. Enjoy the sunshine. Maybe take a little swim in the river. Cool off." The white parishioners left quickly, glancing just briefly at the trio huddled together at the edge of the last bench. The Indians waited for the white people to leave, then slowly stood and exited the chapel.

Alone now in the chapel Claudia, Mary, and Joe sat quietly for several minutes. Finally, Claudia stood and wrapped her arms around Mary's heaving shoulders. Once Mary stopped crying, she looked up and said quietly, "I am sorry. Let us leave here." They stood and walked slowly out of the chapel toward the bridge and the Indian lodges.

A short time later Old Joe, sitting on his little stool, could be heard strumming some gentle chords on his guitar in front of the lodge where Mary and Claudia rested.

## 20
## Fort Laramie

All of the following week Mary White Eagle ventured from the lodge she shared with Claudia Red Deer only to work the evening meals in the dining hall. Claudia, or one of the other Cheyenne women, and once an older Arapaho woman, carried coffee and food to her for breakfast. Neither did she visit her mother's grave, though not to do so pained her deeply. She had promised her mother's spirit that she would tend her grave site weekly, cleaning it and bringing fresh flowers, but as the small Indian cemetery was on the hill behind the fort she feared encountering Father Shannon anywhere she walked. She felt revulsion where he had twice touched her, and often at night as she prepared for bed she vigorously scrubbed her left shoulder as if to remove a stain. Over several nights, as she lay on her bedding in the lodge, she imagined that he may have had more than a spiritual interest in her. She wrapped a blanket tightly around her body, and curled into a fetal position as if to protect her privacy.

§

After several days of cloudy, wet weather, about six o'clock on the morning of July 30, the sun exploded from behind seemingly impervious clouds. Light danced down the length of Laramie River and caressed the fort's many buildings, including the Indian lodges. Claudia Red Deer quickly exited her lodge and proclaimed to the whole Indian village "Ese'he Ohme'ehnestse, the sun is rising." She thrust her head inside the lodge and called, "Mary White Eagle, come outside. Be a Hoxehetane, a sun dancer. Come out now, Voaxaa'ohvo'komaestse. He'kono'ta, stand strong!"

Mary stepped out of the lodge and gazed at the brilliant sunlight suddenly festooning the early morning air. "Yes," she cried to Claudia, "The sun is here. Let us dance, Ma'o vaotseva!" She grasped Claudia's hands and together they began whirling around in circles, kicking their heels high and swinging their entwined arms wildly in the air. The more ground they covered and the more joyous their shouts of "Look, nes hoxeha'e, two sun-dance women," the more infectious their movements and shouts became. More Cheyenne women and some from different tribes, including Arapaho and Lakota, emerged from their lodges and began dancing wildly across the field. Braves and a few older Indian men emerged from their lodges and looked baffled at the numerous women joyfully whirling together in ever-widening circles before the Indian encampment. "The sun-dance is for men," an older Cheyenne man shouted. "Women, what are you doing?"

"Ese' he Ohme' ehnestse! Ese' he Ohme' ehnestse!" Mary White Eagle proclaimed. "The rising sun! The rising sun is here! And we are Hoxehetane'o, sun dancers, and Hoxeha'e, sun-dance women. He'kono'ta, we stand strong. Cheyenne women are strong!"

"Yes," Claudia Red Deer shouted, "A'ene'xoveva, forever! A'ene'xoveva! Right, Voaxaa'ohvo'komaestse?"

"Yes, Ma'o vaotseva. A'ene'xoveva!"

The women twirled together for several minutes before collapsing in small groups on the field, laughing heartily and gesturing toward the steadily rising sun. "Memestatamao'o, seseatamao'o," they shouted amid uncontrollable laughter. "Hoxeha'e, hoxeha'e," the women chanted, and fell backward and raised their arms toward the sky, shouting "oestone'tov ese'he!" One of the soldiers who had heard the women's giddy laughter and watched their dancing frenzy spread around the encampment turned to a Cheyenne brave and asked what the women were saying.

"You really want to know?" the brave asked.

"Yes, I do," the soldier replied.

"Well, in Cheyenne the women are saying that they offer themselves to the sun and that they are laughing so hard that they are farting and peeing on themselves. That's how happy they are when they dance with the sun. Usually Cheyenne men perform the sun dance for the whole tribe, but today the women are dancing. Not sure exactly what started all this, but something made them very happy to see the sun after so many cloudy days. We heard about something in the chapel with Mary White Eagle last week. But I don't know much beyond that. Maybe ask one of the women dancers. I don't know if white women can ever be that happy. But it is very hard for Indian people, men or women, to be happy in this fort. So I guess something made them real happy to see the sun come out this morning."

"Hmmm," the soldier mused, "must be something really special. Hope they enjoyed themselves. And you're right. Real hard for anyone to be happy in this place. Well, see you around," the soldier replied.

"Sure," the brave responded. "See you around."

One hour later most of the older women were resting in their lodges while many younger women walked across the bridge toward the cluster of buildings on the other side. Mary White Eagle held Claudia Red Deer's hand as they walked together toward the dining area where they would serve breakfast.

§

At a little past noon that day two men on horseback rode into the Indian encampment. The older man, dressed in clean, new attire—buffalo moccasins, buckskin pants, a cotton shirt, and black leather vest adorned with images of buffalos and eagles—sat straight in his saddle and wore a full head dress of eagle feathers. The younger man was dressed more modestly in faded denim pants and shirt and weathered leather boots. They stopped when a Cheyenne brave approached them and grabbed the reins of the elder rider's horse.

"Hello, welcome. You are new here I believe. I take by your head dress you are Cheyenne, right? Do you have people here? Are you looking for someone? Who are you?"

"I am Nahkohemahta' sooma. This is my young companion, Johnny Redarrow. He has just an English name so far. We seek Voaxaa'ohvo'komaestse, he'evoehne'e Hotoa' oxhaa' estaestse, Ve'ohtsemosane. Mary White Eagle, the daughter of Tall Bull. She must now journey with us far away. Masetanov, please, where can we find her?"

"Her lodge is just down this trail, where there's several Cheyenne people together. She lives with Ma'o Vaotseva, another Cheyenne woman," the brave said. "There's a big nesenohevooma covering the entrance."

"Ah, yes, a two-colored blanket. How appropriate. We will look for her lodge now. Nea' ese."

"Masetsestov, Nahkohemahta' sooma," the brave said, and released the horse's reins and walked away.

"Nesemoo'o, what did he say?"

"He said 'You are welcome, Spirit Bear.' You have much Cheyenne to learn. His is good. Come, let's find Voaxaa'ohvo'komaestse."

## 21
## Passing

Moments later the riders stopped a short distance from Mary White Eagle's lodge. Nesemoo'o dismounted and approached the blanket draped over the entrance.

"Hello, anybody home?" he called.

"Who is asking?" came a voice from within.

"Nesemoo'o, Spirit Guide. I come searching for Voaxaa'ohvo'komaestse, Mary White Eagle."

She burst from the lodge and stared at Nesemoo'o. "You know my Cheyenne name! Where are you from? How did you get here? Why are you here now?"

"Many questions, all in English! Yes, I know your Cheyenne name. I rode here over many days with my companion Johnny Redarrow, the young man there sitting on his horse. More about him in a moment. I am here because you and I must talk, and because you and Johnny Redarrow must go on a very long journey together, and it is almost time to start. You ask where I am from. As I told Redarrow when he asked me that question many days ago, I am from the past, from memory. Me'etano'ta, I remember what must not be lost."

Mary White Eagle gasped, cupped her hands over her mouth, and stepped back. For several seconds she stared in utter belief at Nesemoo'o. "I... Can this be? Are you real?"

"Yes, I am real. Do not doubt what you see and hear. I am Nahkohemahta' sooma."

"Nahkohemahta' sooma, mo hoxovehne na ovaxestotse. Spirit Bear, you have walked across my dreams. And now you have come. You are here!"

"Yes, I am here. And now you must meet my companion."

Nesemoo'o turned to Redarrow. "Johnny, get off that horse and meet Voaxaa'ohvo'komaestse. You have memorized her name, right, as I said you must?"

Redarrow dismounted, approached her, and extended his right hand. "Hello, Voaxaa..., uh, Mary White Eagle. Sorry, I need to practice. I am pleased to meet you. Nesemoo'o has told me that we must travel a very long way together and be in sacred ceremonies. And he has prepared me for what we must do."

"Yes, in my dreams I have seen all this," Mary White Eagle said. "Long ago my mother told me that the Cheyenne nation could not be conquered until the hearts of all its women were on the ground. She believed that the Cheyenne spirit could rise again, and for that to happen the Sacred Arrows must be renewed. She said because I am the daughter of one of the last Cheyenne chiefs, Tall Bull, I might be part of that. And so now it seems I will be."

"Yes, you will. You must," replied Nesemoo'o. "You and this young man, the son of Johnny Redfeather, who believed in Maheo and prayed to him at his cabin in the mountains. He will ask to be accepted as a pledge for the Sacred Arrows ceremony. And you must accompany him, just as Sweet Medicine had a woman for his companion when he went to the Sacred Mountain. Mamoheve-mo, you two together."

As Mary White Eagle was about to respond, she heard Claudia Red Deer calling her name and saw Claudia running toward her. When she reached Mary, she called out, "Mary White Eagle, oh Mary! Old Joe is dead!"

"What? Old Joe? Claudia, what happened?"

"He died about an hour ago, up in the dining area. He was just sitting there, drinking a cup of coffee, and he suddenly dropped the cup and died right there. It's so sad." Then seeing the visitors, she added, "Oh, sorry, I didn't mean to interrupt."

"It's all right. Claudia, this is Johnny Redarrow and his Cheyenne guide, Nesemoo'o. Friends, meet Ma'o'vaotseva, Claudia Red Deer, who lives with me in our lodge."

"Hello," Claudia responded. "Welcome. You are Cheyenne?"

"Yes, we are Cheyenne. Mostly," Nesemoo'o responded, glancing at Redarrow.

"Friends, the man Claudia just mentioned everyone here called 'Old Joe' who has been kind to us and used to play his guitar for us and the travelers here at the fort." Mary White Eagle turned to Claudia. "Oh this is awful. I am so sorry," she said.

"Yes, I know. The poor old man. He was just so alone most of the time here. But he was kind, and loved to play his guitar. So sweet. I just saw Major Cramer. He wants Joe buried soon, tomorrow or maybe the next day. I told him that we would want to be at any burial service."

"Yes, of course," Mary White Eagle said. She turned to Nesemoo'o. "Claudia and I must do this. You understand. We will find a lodge for you both to stay for a few days. I just can't think of leaving right away."

"Leaving?" Claudia asked. "Are you leaving Mary? Whatever for?"

"Claudia, I will explain later. For now, let us visit Major Cramer. We need to make the arrangements for Old Joe's burial. Maybe a service. Nesemoo'o, you and Redarrow can stay here in our lodge to rest. We will return after we have spoken to the Major."

"Of course, " Nesemoo'o replied. "We will wait here for you. Nea'ese. Thank you."

## 22
## Light

Three nights later Nesemoo'o, Johnny Redarrow, Mary White Eagle, and Claudia Red Deer sat quietly around a small fire pit outside the women's lodge. The last of the kindling that Claudia Red Dear had tossed into the fire crackled as she used a stick to push the pieces together. The kindling flamed, suddenly illuminating the four faces staring into the fire and increasing momentarily its warmth. Mary White Dear drew her shawl more tightly around her shoulders. "Chilly at night out here," she remarked, and leaned closer to Claudia Red Dear.

"Ma'o'vaotseva, Voaxaa'ohvo'komaestse, tell me please why this man you called Old Joe was so important to you," Nesemoo'o said.

"Well," Mary White Eagle began, "I am not sure when he arrived at the fort, but he came up to me a few days after I buried my mother and offered to play for me. I guess he thought that his playing might comfort me. He was just really kind that way. Never rude. He was with me and Claudia on the Sunday nearly two weeks ago when Father Shannon, a priest here, tried to instruct me with his 'preaching' about the Gospel and Jesus. He touched me and I got very angry and told him never to do that again. Later Old Joe came by our lodge and sat down on his stool and just played for us. He was trying to calm us I guess. I think he understood why I was so angry. And you know, he said something really beautiful to me. He said...."

Mary White Eagle paused, and turned to Nesemoo'o. "He said sometimes the spirit might find you, or you might find it, just when you don't expect it. And he said that's why Indians and black folks had to keep believing and praying. Strange I should remember that now. Nesemoo'o, Spirit Guide, you have come when I did not expect you, even though you, or someone like you, has often been in my dreams. And you have found me. Old Joe was right about that. Maybe he was a wise man, a kind of spiritual leader, like you. Maybe he had visions or dreams too. Who knows?"

Mary White Eagle rose suddenly and dashed into her lodge. She emerged several minutes later holding a small wooden hoop wrapped tightly in tan leather straps. Attached to the top of the hoop were two more strands bound together to form a handle. Inside the hoop very thin leather strips, some inserted through tiny blue beads, tied to the outer hoop and also to each other in circular patterns, forming an intricate spider's web, or net, surrounding a small central opening. Dangling from the bottom were seven more leather straps doubled over the hoop and squeezed at their end through red beads and pinching small eagle feathers. Nesemoo'o smiled when Mary White Eagle held the decorated hoop aloft.

"What is that?" Redarrow asked.

"That," she said, "is for catching ovaxe, dreams. Many tribes of the plains and mountains make them. They have their own designs and colors. This one is Ojibwe. My mother got it from a woman in North Dakota many years ago, when she was a young girl, and she gave this to me just before she died and told me to keep it with me forever. We will take it with us tomorrow. It will catch bad dreams so they do not harm us, and let good dreams we will need for our journey to come through to us."

"Voaxaa'ohvo'komaestse, you have done well to tell Johnny Redarrow of the dream catcher. I did not know that you had one, but I am very pleased that you do. Yes, we will carry it with us for all of our journey."

"Nea'ese, thank you, Nesemoo'o."

"Masetsesta, you are welcome. And you know," Nesemoo'o replied, "maybe Old Joe really was like Indian elders, wise in ways other people do not understand. One who speaks truth that their people must believe. You see, his prophecy has come true. I, Nahkohemahta' sooma, Spirit Bear, have found you when you did not expect me. It is good that you stayed for his burial, and that it was done properly. I imagine his spirit, like your mother's, is at rest after its journey. And now we must go on ours, with Johnny Redarrow here, who still has not found his tongue. Have you Johnny?"

"No, I have not. Nor do I know when I will. Nesemoo'o, you have said that you are from memory. I have no such memory as you have of the Cheyenne, or of my father. I believe that I sensed his spirit up at his cabin, but I can't say much more right now about that or anything else. All I remember is Evanston, and the white man's dirty machines. Maybe on this journey I shall now learn enough about being Cheyenne to someday have such a memory."

"I trust you shall," Nesemoo'o added.

Mary White Eagle took Claudia's hands in hers and looked straight into her eyes. "Ma'o vahkotseva, you understand why I have to leave tomorrow, don't you? You know about the Sacred Arrows, and the renewal ceremonies. I have dreamed of a wise elder who would come to me about a journey and the sacred ceremonies. When I told my mother about these dreams, she told me not to doubt them, and to wait. I can only say that I have felt this need, this call, coming to me for many months now. Maybe longer. Johnny Redarrow will ask to be accepted as a pledge and I must go with him, just as Sweet Medicine was accompanied by a woman long ago when he went to the Sacred Mountain. Our people are suffering, and their spirit must be renewed. And for that to happen Johnny Redarrow and I must go on this journey to the Cheyenne reservation in Oklahoma. It is not pretty, nor is it a good place for our people. But we must pray to Maheo, the Holy One, and with the Sacred Arrows ceremony raise up the spirit of the Cheyenne people. We will ride tomorrow with the sun."

"And I?" Claudia Red Deer asked.

"Ma'o vahkotseva, do not fear for yourself," Nesemoo'o said quietly. "You will be here with other Cheyenne and Lakota people, and you will be well. I promise you that."

Mary put her arm around Claudia's shoulder. "Claudia, remember what our mothers have said to us: the hearts of Cheyenne women, our hearts, must not be left to die on the ground." She hugged Claudia tightly. "Look up. There is some moon light tonight, not much, just a crescent, but it is growing. We will travel south and follow the path of the sun across the sky, and every night the moon will bring us more light until we arrive at the reservation. And that will be wonderful, for us and for all Cheyenne people. But now this little fire is dying, and we must sleep before our journey begins tomorrow. So come, let us rest. Nesemoo'o and Johnny Redarrow, Pehevetaa'eva, good night." She and Claudia Red Deer rose and walked into their lodge.

"Pehevetaa'eva," Nesemoo'o added.

Nesemoo'o and Johnny Redarrow sat a few moments longer, staring into the fading fire. "Come, Johnny, we too must rest for our journey. And early tomorrow we must see Major Cramer for the provisions he has kindly promised us. You must find your tongue tomorrow. We will have much to say to one another. Are you all right?"

"Yes, Nesemoo'o, I am all right. Just still a bit unsure about this journey we must go on. It all still seems so strange."

"Strange and wonderful. You will see." They rose and walked several yards to a lodge near the river. Nesemoo'o went inside immediately, but Redarrow lingered outside, then walked slowly to the river. He knelt on one knee and looked up at the trillions of lights blazing above the wilderness. "Oh my father, Johnny Redfeather," he whispered, "where among the stars is your cabin now? Teach me to find it whenever I look up. Is your spirit at peace there? Are you pleased that I am going on this journey tomorrow? Perhaps you know what will become of me, of the Cheyenne people? Perhaps I too will know when I arrive at our destination."

He bowed his head. "Listen, my father. Listen! Come with me. Let us go together. Please!" He remained kneeling for several minutes, then rose and walked slowly back to his lodge.

"You have been praying, haven't you?" Nesemoo'o asked once Johnny was lying near him.

"Yes. How did you know?"

"I just know. Sleep now, Ma Maahetaneve."

"Who? Now what?"

"Your name in Cheyenne. Man of the Red Arrow, one who worships the Sacred Arrows. Your mother named you well. You will get a new name at the ceremony, so learn this in Cheyenne and enjoy it while you can."

"Nesemoo'o, will I ever see my mother again? I promised Courtney I would return to her."

"Eventually, yes. First, we must travel, and you must offer yourself as a pledge for the Sacred Arrows Ceremony. Now, you must sleep. The way is long."

## 23
### Departure

At sunrise on Sunday, August 4 Nahkohemahta'sooma, Voaxaa'ohvo'komaestse, and Ma Maahetaneve slowly guided their horses due east past the Indian lodges and settlers' encampments toward the primitive wagon road that led into the fort. When they reached the road they turned right and began their long journey south to the Cheyenne reservation in Oklahoma Territory. They would ride for many days following the path of the sun, and each night the silvery brightness of the waxing moon blessed their journey.

In his saddle bag Ma Maahetaneve carried his father's four arrows wrapped securely in a leather satchel. He would present these to Hah Ke' and ask to be accepted as a pledge for the Sacred Arrows Ceremony. When asked why he wished to pledge, he would answer because he is the son of Johnny Redfeather, who believed in Maheo in his cabin in the mountains, and because the time to do so has arrived.

## Epilogue

We must invent overnight, figuratively speaking, another kind of civilization, one more cognizant of limits, less greedy, more compassionate, less bigoted, more inclusive, less exploitative.
—Barry Lopez, *Embrace Fearlessly the Burning World*

## Postscript

The Green River Trilogy begins with a violent attack on Milly's Green River Saloon on September 22, 1866, and concludes on August 4, 1889 as Spirit Guide leads his party away from Fort Laramie and toward the Cheyenne reservation in Oklahoma. Though steeped in history, these books are fictional, and Seotse (Spirit) is clearly visionary. However, the ceremony that it imagines at the end of Johnny Redarrow's demanding journey is central to the spiritual life of the Cheyenne. I conclude this trilogy with a profound prayer from the Sacred Arrows Ceremony performed on the Cheyenne reservation in Cantonment, Oklahoma in Fall, 1908. This prayer was spoken by Bull Thigh, a Northern Suhtai priest:

"Great Father, my Grandfather, have mercy on me.
My Grandfather, allow me to live happy alone, away from harm. Grandfather, have mercy on me that I may live as long as the evergreen trees; that I may live to see the ancient hills, the ancient air. Grandfather, give us abundant food, to live higher and higher without harm. Grandfather, our Creator, give us strength to live in holiness. Grandfather, place us in direct life and guide us directly to the end. Grandfather, bless and pity us in our earth, in our existence. Thou art holy. Thou art mighty, who placed us on this earth."

What began in violence ends in prayer.

# REFERENCES

Historical information found in this novel comes from the following sources:

Berthrong, Donald J, *The Southern Cheyenne*. Norman: University of Oklahoma Press, 1963

*WWW.Cheyennelanguage.org.*

Cozzens, Peter, *The Earth is Weeping: the Epic Story of the Indian Wars for the American West*. New York: Alfred A. Knopf, 2016

DeLoria, Jr. Vine, *God Is Red*. New York: Dell Publishing, 1973

Grinnell, George Bird, *By Cheyenne Campfires*. 1926. Rpt: New Haven and London: Yale University Press, 1962

Grinnell, George Bird. *The Cheyenne Indians; Their History and Ways of Life*. 2 vols. New Haven: Yale University Press, 1923

———. George Bird, *The Fighting Cheyenne*. Norman: University of Oklahoma Press, 1956

———. George Bird. "The Great Mysteries of the Cheyenne." *American Anthropologist* Vol 12 # 4; New Series (Oct.-Dec. 1910): 542-75

———. George Bird, "Some Early Cheyenne Tales." *The Journal of American Folklore* Vol. 20 # 78 (July-Sept. 1907): 169-94

Hyde, George E., *Spotted Tail's Folk*. 1961; rev. ed., Norman: University of Oklahoma Press, 1974

John Stands in Timber and Margot Liberty, *Cheyenne Memories*. 1967; Rpt. Lincoln: University of Nebraska Press, 1972.

McChristian, Douglas C. *Fort Laramie: Military Bastion of the High Plains*. Norman, OK: The Arthur H. Clark Company, 2008.

Powell, Peter J., *People of the Sacred Mountain: A History of the Northern Cheyenne Chiefs and Warrior Societies*, 1830-1879. 2 vols. New York: Harper & Row, 1981

——— Peter J., *Sweet Medicine: The Continuing Role of the Sacred Arrows and the Sacred Buffalo Hat in Northern Cheyenne History*. 2 vols. Norman: University of Oklahoma Press, 1969

Seotse, Cheyenne for Spirit

# Readers Guide

1. The word "Seotse" in Cheyenne means "Spirit." This is a complex word in any language; all cultures use it in theological, psychological, political, and personal contexts. We speak of the "spiritual elements" of a religion; the "spirit" of an athletic team, such as a high school football team; we say a politician gave a "spirited speech"; and we say that a friend or our spouse has a "spirited [i.e. lively] personality." Discuss thoroughly the ways in which "spirit" is used in this novel; who uses the word; for what purposes; and how do the various speakers intend their use of the word to affect other people? Where, for example, do characters use the word in what we might term a "cross-cultural" sense?

2. Consult some of the historical sources used in this novel, especially Peter Cozzens's *The Earth is Weeping*, to more fully understand the tragic history of the Cheyenne Indians, especially in the mid to late nineteenth century. How does this history affect your understanding of Mary White Eagle and Johnny Redarrow in the novel?

3. Although Old Joe appears in only a few scenes, in what ways might one argue that his presence is crucial to Mary White Eagle's recovery from her mother's death and her later decision to accompany Johnny Redarrow to the Cheyenne renewal ceremony in Oklahoma? What is Joe's sense of "spirit," and how has his history influenced what might be called his "faith in the spirit?" An important critical question in analyzing any work of literature, regardless of its genre, is "What would be lost if X [character, scene, etc.] were eliminated?" What would be lost from Seotse if Old Joe were not there? Examine this analogy: Old Joe is

to Mary White Eagle as Spirit Guide is to Johnny Redarrow. (Remember that the white people of Evanston call Spirit Guide "Old Indian.")

4. Examine carefully the crucial conversation between Mary White Eagle and Father Shannon in chapter three. How does each character use the word "spirit?" What is similar, but also different, about how each character uses the word? What does each not grasp about the other's understanding of "spirit?" How is this conversation an important harbinger of the crucial scene in the chapel (chapter 19) when Mary White Eagle finally decides to attend the Catholic Mass?

5. In the first two books of the Green River Trilogy, *Green River Saga* (2020) and *Raven Mountain: A Mythic Tale* (2023), Milly's Green River Saloon is the centerpiece. What is the symbolism of Johnny Redarrow's deciding not to enter the saloon in Evanston after Spirit Guide confronts him on the boardwalk?

6. Nesemoo'o, or Spirit Guide, is both a real physical character and a spiritual guide for Johnny Redarrow. He knows a great deal about Redarrow's father, Johnny Redfeather, who is the principal character in *Raven Mountain*. There is a clear explanation in the scene at Redfeather's cabin on Raven Mountain of how Nesemoo'o knows certain facts about Redfeather, but where in the novel does Nesemoo'o possess what can only be called supernatural knowledge? How does this knowledge contribute to your understanding of the title of the novel as well as the complexity of Nesemoo's character? Can he be both a "real" and a "spiritual" character in the various landscapes, or settings, of the novel? In which of these settings does his dual identity seem most convincing?

7. At the heart of *Seotse* is one of the most common and complex motifs in all of world literature: the search for the father. This motif occurs in plays as different as Sophocles's *Oedipus Rex* and Shakespeare's *Hamlet*, and Freud has firmly implanted the Oedipal Complex in the Western mind. (Like Hamlet at the end of the ghost scene early in Shakespeare's play, in the final chapter Redarrow asks his father to go with him on his journey.) How does an understanding of this literary motif contribute to your grasp of the structure of *Seotse* and your understanding of both main characters: Johnny Redarrow and Mary White Eagle?

8. Another approach to the book's structure is via Joseph Campbell's important book *The Hero With A Thousand Faces*. Look especially at Campbell's diagram "The Keys" at the beginning of chapter four, "The Hero's Adventure." Campbell outlines the essential features of the archetypal journey that all heroes in all cultures must embrace. For Johnny Redarrow, the "Call to Adventure" obviously occurs outside the saloon in Evanston. Using Campbell's diagram, explain the functions of several of the minor characters in *Seotse* and their contributions to the final journeys undertaken by Johnny Redarrow and Mary White Eagle.

9. Chapter 19, the scene in the small chapel at Fort Laramie, is obviously crucial to the entire novel. Examine this scene very carefully. First, what are Fr. Shannon's motives for inviting Mary White Eagle to Mass? Remember that he is a Catholic priest who believes that "outside the Church there is no salvation," a central tenet of traditional Roman Catholicism. Second, why is he so insistent that she come to Mass? When the night before he prays that God will help him "secure her for my righteous ministry," what does he mean? Near the end of his sermon he walks to Mary White Eagle's pew and gently touches her shoulder. Why does he do this, and why does Mary White Eagle react as she does? Is her reaction justified? Recall the epigraph from Dostoyevsky's chapter "The Grand Inquisitor"; how is it relevant to *Seotse*?

10. In *Raven Mountain* Johnny Redfeather explains to his lover Courtney Dillard the story of Sweet Medicine, the central figure of the Cheyenne creation narrative. Research this narrative, which can be done quickly online and in numerous books about the Cheyenne people, and explain how Sweet Medicine and his story are central to *Seotse*.

11. *Seotse* concludes the Green River Trilogy, The first book is *Green River Saga* (2020), and the second is *Raven Mountain: A Mythic Tale* (2023). Considering the historical information in these three novels about the Northern and Southern Cheyenne Indians, even though this history is presented in fictional contexts, evaluate the conclusion of *Seotse*, including the prayer from an actual Cheyenne renewal ceremony that concludes the novel. Is this ending satisfactory? Whimsical? Too Brief? Fitting for a series of historical novels?